MW01134170

SWEETS

GALORE

Connie Shelton

Books
by Connie Shelton

THE CHARLIE PARKER SERIES
Deadly Gamble
Vacations Can Be Murder
Partnerships Can Be Murder
Small Towns Can Be Murder
Memories Can Be Murder
Honeymoons Can Be Murder
Reunions Can Be Murder
Competition Can Be Murder
Balloons Can Be Murder
Obsessions Can Be Murder
Gossip Can Be Murder
Stardom Can Be Murder
Phantoms Can Be Murder
Buried Secrets Can Be Murder
Legends Can Be Murder

Holidays Can Be Murder - a Christmas novella

THE SAMANTHA SWEET SERIES
Sweet Masterpiece
Sweet's Sweets
Sweet Holidays
Sweet Hearts
Bitter Sweet
Sweets Galore
Sweets, Begorra
Sweet Payback
Sweet Somethings
Sweets Forgotten
The Woodcarver's Secret

SWEETS GALORE

The Sixth Samantha Sweet Mystery

Connie Shelton

Secret Staircase Books

Sweets Galore
Published by Secret Staircase Books, an imprint of
Columbine Publishing Group
PO Box 416, Angel Fire, NM 87710

Copyright © 2013 Connie Shelton
All rights reserved. No part of this book may be reproduced or
transmitted in any form or by any means, electronic or mechanical,
including photocopying, recording, or by an information storage and
retrieval system without permission in writing from the publisher.

Printed and bound in the United States of America
ISBN 1482772434
ISBN-13 978-1482772432

This book is a work of fiction. Names, characters, places and
incidents are either the product of the author's imagination or are
used fictitiously. Any resemblance to actual events or locales or
persons, living or dead, is entirely coincidental. Although the author
and publisher have made every effort to ensure the accuracy and
completeness of information contained in this book we assume
no responsibility for errors, inaccuracies, omissions, or any
inconsistency herein. Any slights of people, places or organizations
are unintentional.

Book layout and design by Secret Staircase Books
Cover illustration © Dmitry Maslov
Cover cupcake design © Makeitdoubleplz

First trade paperback edition: March, 2013
First e-book edition: March, 2013

*For Dan, who has made my life
special and wonderful.*

My thanks go out to Susan Slater; the books are always better with your editorial touches. And of course to all my readers—I keep writing them for you!

Chapter 1

Samantha Sweet stood before her full-length mirror. Champagne silk, with ivory lace insets, the tiered skirt that skimmed the floor, the tiny rows of pearls—so beautiful. Except for the way the fabric puckered around her midsection. She moaned in frustration.

"This fit perfectly six months ago. What happened?"

Her friend, Rupert Penrick, tugged at the two halves of the zipper but they were inches away from meeting in the back. "It's just a little off. And it's late in the day. Everyone gets a little puffy late in the day."

"I'm getting married in the afternoon," Sam said. "In one week. How am I ever going to manage this?"

Kelly's eyes met Sam's in the mirror, then edged away to look at the errant zipper. "Ooh."

"I know this fabulous spa in Santa Fe," Rupert said. "A week there and you'll drop those pounds like magic."

"Mom, I don't want to sound like a downer here but dropping twenty pounds in a week is going to take more than a steady diet of carrot sticks. I'll get you a guest membership at my gym."

How could I have let this happen? She turned sideways to get a look at the hopeless situation. This dress had been a perfect fit back in February when she and Beau originally planned their wedding at Valentine's Day. But the inevitable delay—due to circumstances beyond her control—stress, not watching her diet, the temptations of all those baked goodies right there in front of her every day . . . She stood tall and sucked in her breath but there was no way the zipper would close, not without drastic action.

"At least veils don't have sizes," Kelly offered, holding up the froth of tulle that matched the champagne tone of the dress.

"That doesn't help," Sam said, although she knew the veil would look good now that she'd let her short hair grow out a little. "Okay, let me get back into my other clothes. I'll have to figure out something."

She shooed the others out of her bedroom and peeled the dress down over her hips. A dozen possibilities flitted through her mind: wear something else for the wedding, have this dress altered, starve for a week and then hold her breath through the ceremony.

The one thing she could *not* do was to postpone the wedding again. Beau would start to wonder how serious she really was about their marriage, and that would be bad enough, but her mother would kill her.

After pressing Sam to set the date this past summer, Nina Rae had reinforced her troops with relatives from all over the place. Members of the Sweet family from Texas, Colorado and Oklahoma were congregating in Taos next weekend and there *would* be a wedding.

Sam let out a sigh and slipped into jeans and a loose blouse. When she walked into the kitchen Kelly was pouring hot water over a tea bag in a cup.

"Here, this is supposed to reduce water retention," she said, handing the cup to Sam. "Rupert had to go. Said he's on some kind of deadline with his editor."

Rupert Penrick secretly wrote steamy romance novels under the pen name Victoria Devane and downplayed the fact that he was perpetually on the bestseller lists.

Sam had frequently wondered what Victoria's readers would think if they knew the pink-clad blonde in the author photos was a model and that the real writer was a male nearly six feet tall with flowing gray collar-length hair who, at two-twenty, filled a room wearing his signature blousy purple shirts and scarves that probably cost what Sam earned in a week. At least he usually offered sound fashion advice.

She debated actually taking him up on the offer to visit that Santa Fe spa, but instantly discarded it. Even if she could afford the place—which was doubtful—there was no way she could take the next week off from her two jobs. Between breaking into houses and running a bakery, life was running at full speed right now.

She looked up at Kelly. "I need to teach you the finer points of picking locks," she said, "just in case a new assignment comes along. I haven't been away for two straight weeks since I took that job."

Kelly looked a little apprehensive.

"Mostly, we're going to winterize my current three properties, in case the weather turns colder before I get back. There probably won't be anything new. You'll handle it just fine."

"And I can call you if I really hit a snag, right? I mean, you'll be driving during the days, stopping at night. You could offer the voice of experience if I need it."

"I'm going on my honeymoon. I'm really hoping not to hear from either you or Jen the whole time."

Jennifer Baca, one of her bakery employees, could easily handle the customers in any typical week. With Julio baking and Becky decorating, Sam didn't foresee anything her team couldn't manage at Sweet's Sweets.

Sam's and Beau's plan to take a leisurely driving trip through the Southwest was their ideal getaway—no pressure to meet a schedule, beautiful autumn scenery in southern Colorado and Arizona, and time simply to enjoy themselves. No crimes to solve for the handsome sheriff of Taos County.

"We won't bother you, Mom. If Jen runs into a problem at the bakery, I'm sure Riki will let me take some time away from the pooches to go help her out."

Kelly was a lot better at bathing dogs than at decorating cakes, but Sam didn't say anything. She'd been telling herself for months now that everything would work out all right. She glanced at the clock above the stove.

"There's time to make it to the place on Bowen Road

before dark," she told Kelly. "We might as well get it out of the way."

Kelly picked up a notepad that always sat near the phone. "I better write stuff down."

Sam nodded. Even at thirty-four, her curly-haired daughter had her scatter-brained moments. Last year at this time she'd arrived in Taos to inform Sam that she'd quit her job and lost her home in California to foreclosure while racking up a ton of credit card debt. At least she'd fiscally settled down quite a bit since she'd been here.

Ten minutes later they were walking the perimeter of a modest adobe, not unlike Sam's own house, on a quiet street near the center of town.

"We'll shut off the water supply and put anti-freeze in the drains, since this place has had the power cut off. Without heat—"

"The pipes would freeze," Kelly finished. "See? I am getting some of this stuff."

"Good. I'm just reminding, since years in southern California couldn't give you a clue about how early in the season we get freezing temps here in the mountains."

They circled the house, disconnecting garden hoses and stowing them in the garage. Indoors, Sam went through the rooms, showed Kelly what to do, how to fill out the required sign-in sheet and stash the key back in the lock box at the front door.

"If you don't have to get home to Beau, how about some dinner?" Kelly suggested as they drove away. "I'll spring for pizza."

Sam gave her a hard look.

"Oh, yeah. How about a salad?"

"I better just get out to Beau's place. Our place." Why did she have such a hard time, still, calling Beau's large house her home? The acreage, the horses, two loving dogs, the warm glow of the log walls when the lamps were low and the fireplace blazing—it was an idyllic spot. And Beau. The first man in her life who loved her unconditionally, completely, committed but without an agenda for changing her or uprooting her life.

After dropping Kelly off she drove north, passing the turnoff to the Taos Pueblo and a string of little businesses, then made the familiar turn toward the mountains and drove through the big stone gateway to the property.

Home, she said to herself. *Home, home, home*. Nellie and Ranger came to attention on the covered wooden porch, recognized her red pickup truck and sat expectantly as she parked next to her bakery van and walked toward them. Beau was working late tonight and the black Lab and the smaller border collie wouldn't be entirely comfortable until he arrived and completed the family circle. Nevertheless, both greeted Sam effusively, tails whipping back and forth, nudging and pressing against her legs in competition for her attention.

She indulged them in a brisk rubdown and checked their food bowls. "I'm not feeding you guys until I check with your daddy," she said. Nellie, particularly, would eat six times a day if someone let her do it.

Sam let herself inside and spent a moment staring at the late afternoon view from the French doors that led to a back deck and looked out over the open pasture land beyond. The tall cottonwoods that bordered Beau's acreage were hitting their full yellow-gold splendor and the grasses had already begun to go brown with the cooler nights.

She switched on lamps in the living room, where Western art and Indian blankets decorated the walls. Beau had told her to change anything she wanted, to add a woman's touch. But Sam honestly admired his taste in the furnishings and knew that nothing from her old house could compare in quality. She would leave her old things behind as long as Kelly wanted to stay in their smaller house in the middle of town.

Beyond the windows, darkness set in quickly and Sam went to the kitchen to see what she might make for a solo dinner. Kelly's suggestion of salad made sense, and the fridge was well stocked so she chopped a few leaves of lettuce and some veggies and tried to resist the dressings.

This isn't so bad, she kept telling herself. *I can handle a week of salads.* She ignored a Sweet's Sweets box of cookies she'd brought home earlier in the week and went to the living room to switch on the television.

Distraction, distraction, she reminded herself. She steered away from the Food Channel and found an old movie where the actors did a lot more talking than eating.

She was dozing on the sofa when she heard sounds outside. Boots on the wooden deck, a gentle voice speaking to the dogs, the front door latch.

"Hey, darlin'. Did I wake you up?"

She covered a yawn by rubbing at her face and running fingers through her hair. "TV. I must have dozed."

He shed his jacket, draping it over an elk antler coat rack near the door, and Sam walked over to hug him from behind.

"Glad you're home," she murmured into his muscular back.

He turned and circled her with his arms, planting a kiss on the top of her head. "Mmm, me too. Did you have a good day?"

"Parts of it were great." She told him about Kelly's little training course in locks and drain pipes, plus the fact that the bakery had run without her help for an entire day.

"Parts of it?" Law enforcement types always seemed to pick up on the little things you don't quite say.

"My wedding gown. It isn't quite the fit it was when I bought it."

"So, wear something else."

Mr. Practical.

"But I love this dress. And there's only going to be one wedding day—ever."

"Have it altered." He held her at arm's length. "Sam, I don't care what you're wearing that day. You know that. I love you. It's an as-is deal."

"Thank you for that. Really. But I'm going to do whatever it takes to get into that dress."

He kissed her, the kind of kiss that can only go one direction and they raced each other up the stairs.

Sam woke the next morning at daylight, with a growl in her stomach. *Dieting is not my strong suit*, she grumbled to herself as she brushed her teeth. *But I can't give up.*

She spat the toothpaste into the sink and gave herself

a little lecture about self discipline and sticking with a plan. Grabbing an apple on her way out the door, she started her bakery van and headed toward town.

The commute, although quite a bit longer than her old one, was much more scenic and she gave herself over to enjoying the rising sun as it hit the fall foliage while she ate her apple. *I will ignore everything sweet or fatty today*, she vowed.

Easy to say, until she got to the bakery and walked in to smell the muffins and scones that Julio had already removed from the oven. She said good morning to the two kitchen employees and braced herself against the temptation to start the day with a croissant and cup of coffee.

"How are the wedding plans coming along?" Becky Harper asked, not looking up from a cake full of flowers upon which she was putting finishing touches.

"Do not let me eat anything," Sam said. "All day."

"Ooh, right. The dress."

Julio sent the women a puzzled look. Sam gave a wan grin. "Don't ask."

He dumped a pitcher full of raw eggs into the big Hobart mixer and switched it on. Sam remembered the first time he'd walked into her shop, how she'd been a little put off by the tattoos that crept from his knuckles to who-knows-where under the white T-shirt, how the rumble of his Harley coming up the alley never failed to startle her just a little. But the guy knew how to bake.

He'd immediately mastered all of Sam's signature recipes and in recent weeks had begun to suggest a few touches of his own. He'd become a real asset to the business, along with Becky as a decorator and Jen keeping the display cases in order.

"After I had my second son," Becky said, "I went on the protein diet. That worked wonders for me."

"With a week to get this done, I think I better be on the water diet," Sam said with a laugh. "But at the moment I need some coffee to wake me up."

She walked through the split in the curtain that separated the kitchen from the sales room, where she found Jen waiting on one of their regulars, a tiny white-haired woman who bought one muffin a day but spent a good thirty minutes choosing it. Jen sent a smile toward Sam. They both knew the woman was just lonely. Sam mouthed a 'thank you' to her assistant for being so patient with her.

Outside the front windows, Sam noticed that the sun had fully lit the store fronts along the way and the parking lot for the little strip of businesses was getting full. A green SUV pulled up to Puppy Chic, and a woman got out with a lanky Irish setter. Kelly and her English-born employer, Erika Davis-Jones, would have their hands full with that one, Sam thought.

To the other side of her own shop Sam saw Ivan Petrenko preparing a table on the sidewalk for his weekly used book sale. She turned to the beverage bar where Jen had set out carafes of their signature blend coffee and hot water for the tea drinkers. She poured coffee into her mug and resisted adding cream, turning her back on the variety of sweeteners and flavors.

A vehicle pulled up directly in front of her shop, a high pickup truck with big tires and shiny chrome wheel rims, and a man got out. He wore jeans with a black turtle-neck and black blazer, and a flash of gold showed at his wrist as he locked the truck. Not from around here, Sam thought. The truck had California plates. Shadows obscured him for a minute as he stepped under her awning, the one that said "Sweet's Sweets" with the slogan "A Bakery of Magical Delights" on a second line.

Tiny bells tinkled as the door opened and the man stepped inside. He gave her an intent stare.

"Hello, Sammy."

She started to ask if she knew him, but the realization hit.

Jake Calendar.

Chapter 2

Sam felt the blood drain from her face. Thirty-five years since she'd seen this man, years that fell away as he gave his familiar grin. He wore his curly brown hair shorter than before, back when they both worked a summer at that pipeline camp in Alaska, but the aquamarine eyes were the same, with a glint of flirtation that lit up his face in every conversation with a female. How gullible she'd been at nineteen.

"You look good, Sammy."

Same old Jake. Same darned old charmer.

"What are you doing here?"

"Hey, what's this? No 'wow, it's good to see you'?" His eyes crinkled as he smiled. *Was that a wink?*

She took a deep breath. "It's actually pretty

unbelievable to see you, Jake. And so I ask again, what on earth are you doing here?"

"Just happened to be in town. Thought I'd look you up."

The elderly lady at the counter paid for her muffin and left. Jen caught Sam's attention, sending a little signal between them, asking if everything was okay. Sam nodded. Jen scurried toward the kitchen, giving Sam a moment to get her thoughts together.

"And just how did you know *where* to look me up?" she asked Jake.

"Online. You can find anyone online these days. Boy, those chocolate cupcakes look amazing. Could I get one of those?"

Damn Facebook, she thought as she went behind the display case and picked up the cupcake he wanted. Why had she listened to Kelly's case for setting up an account so people would know about the bakery?

"And you just *happened* to be in the neighborhood and in the mood for cake?"

"Something like that."

She put on a smile and handed him the chocolate confection, wondering if it were really that simple.

"Sammy, Sammy . . . Can't a couple of old friends just have a cup of coffee together?"

Since her own cup was steaming away, she couldn't very well deny him one as well. She gestured toward the urns and told him to help himself. While he dispensed a cup, she paced to the front door and back. She watched him as he added creamer and sugar.

Still tall and slim, only the slightest touch of gray at the temples, thinner in the face. Not quite as muscular as she remembered, but definitely not gone to fat either. The few wrinkles only added character to his chiseled features. How was it that men aged so much better than women?

As she recalled he'd been only a year or so older than herself, so that would put him at about fifty-four, maybe fifty-five. She couldn't remember when his birthday was—didn't really spend any time thinking about it. She had to admit that he looked good.

He stared steadily at her as he stirred the coffee with a wooden stick. When he grinned it caused one dimple to appear on the left side of his face.

"Sit down, Jake," she said, indicating one of the bistro tables at the side of the room. Her voice came out a lot calmer than she expected. It's only coffee, she told herself. Stop being so resistant. "So? Life has been good to you?"

He sipped at his coffee, complimented her on it. "Pretty good, yeah. You know. Both my parents are gone now. Some wives came and went. I moved around too much, I guess, maybe spent my money a little too freely."

"Sometimes that works with women, sometimes not."

"Huh, yeah. Guess I didn't spend it on the right things."

She eyed the flashy pickup truck outside. "Evidently you bought what you wanted."

He nodded absently, giving the shop a long perusal. "Looks like you're doing real good for yourself."

"Thanks. It was a long road getting here." A series of dead-end jobs, a couple that paid well enough to support herself and her daughter, but realizing the dream of her pastry shop hadn't happened until she met up with a nice windfall last year.

"I tried to find you for a long time, Sammy. You left Alaska real suddenly."

She nodded. "Yeah. Yeah, it was time to move on."

"But you and I . . . we had a pretty hot thing going there." He took an almost sensuous bite from the chocolate cupcake.

A vivid picture came into her mind—a tent camp on the tundra, a down-filled sleeping bag . . . She willed herself not to blush. Wasn't sure if she actually succeeded.

"Jake, I'm about to be married. Even if I once had feelings for you, I'm not looking to rekindle anything."

He held up a hand. "No, Sammy, I didn't expect that. Lot of water under the bridge and all."

"Good. Just so you know. And quit calling me Sammy. Please."

Thoughts churning, Sam sipped at her coffee to avoid saying what she was really thinking or admitting anything that really would be better left unsaid. So many things she'd never told anyone.

She changed the subject. "Jake, it's rare for someone to just *happen* to be in Taos."

He polished off the cupcake in two bites. "All business, right? Well, that's good. I can see that staying businesslike has made you successful."

She waited.

"So, um, there actually is a business reason I've stopped in today." He rolled his cup between his palms as if he needed the warmth. "Like you said, life has been pretty good to me too, recent years. I'm in Hollywood now. You know, the industry. Know a lot of folks out there . . ."

If he expected an answer to that, she couldn't provide the one he wanted. Taos and Santa Fe had their share of Hollywood celebrities—big names and lesser ones—but Sam had never found a whole lot worth knowing in most of those she'd ever met. She'd made it this far in life without needing to cultivate their mostly shallow friendships. She let him fumble a little when the expected star-struck reaction didn't come.

"So, anyway, our current project is a new reality talent show. I know, you're thinking there are already a lot of those—*Idol, The Voice* . . . But Deor has a whole new high-concept approach."

"Dior? Isn't that a fashion designer?"

"D-e-o-r," he spelled it out. "Tustin Deor. You've heard of him, I'm sure. *Wild Kittens, Game Runners* . . ."

He waited but Sam was genuinely drawing a blank.

"So anyway, Tustin and I are scouting New Mexico locations, lining up some partners . . . putting together the whole project, start to finish . . ."

She began to see where this was going. "Are you asking me for money?"

"Sammy—uh, Sam, do you really think I stopped by to see an old friend because I want your money? Please, honey."

She held up a hand. "I'm not 'honey,' Jake. Don't do that. Just take my word for it that I can't invest in any kind of Hollywood project."

He set his empty cup down, reached across the table and took her hands. "This isn't how I wanted this conversation to go, Sam. I really, honestly just wanted to see you again. For old times' sake."

Yeah, right. "Jake, that's nice. It was good to see you. I'm happy for your success in the television business." She pulled her hands back and stood up. "And now I really have work to do."

He leaned back in his chair, and she was afraid he intended to stay awhile, but finally he stood. "Okay, then. I'll be in town for awhile. Staying at the La Fonda, just a couple blocks away. We should have dinner while I'm here."

She wiggled her fingers at him, displaying her engagement ring.

"We could *all* have dinner together," he said.

"We'll see." She stood, he left, and she watched him get into the tricked-out pickup and drive away before she turned toward the kitchen.

She had no intention of bringing up the dinner invitation with Beau. It wasn't like she and Jake had truly been old friends. They were an old item. Two kids working at a pipeline camp, having some fun. One forced to grow up; the other evidently hadn't, even now. She'd very purposefully left him behind and made no effort to stay in touch. Hadn't felt a need to have him in her life.

Besides, she was pretty sure Jake had already covered everything he planned to cover—a little flattery, some fake sentimentality, and cut to the chase with the money request. Now that she'd turned him down, he would surely leave town and go pick on someone else.

"Everything okay, Sam?" Jen asked as they passed each other near the doorway.

"Yeah. A guy I knew ages ago," Sam said.

"He looked kind of familiar. He hasn't come in the shop before?" Jen shrugged it off as two young women came through the front door.

Sam went to the big walk-in fridge to pull out whatever cakes she was supposed to be decorating today. She still needed to get out the sketches for her own wedding cake and be sure to go over them with Julio and Becky. But she found herself staring at the shelves. Jake Calendar looked familiar to Jen because he looked so much like his daughter; Kelly and Jen had known each other since elementary school.

Kelly had never really asked many questions about her missing parent. In these times, so many kids came from single-parent homes that it just wasn't that unusual to have no dad in the picture. She and Sam had formed the perfect little family, all on their own. Even during the terrible-teens, Sam knew she had it easier than a lot of parents whose kids got into real trouble. Kelly might not have been the most responsible kid with her money (another picture of Jake flashed through Sam's mind), but she'd never done drugs or much drinking or picked up any nasty diseases. All in all, Sam felt very lucky.

Over the years Kelly had asked few questions about her father, and she seemed content with Sam's sketchy answers: they'd never been married and the man was not going to be a factor in their lives. Period.

And now Jake had showed up.

Goose bumps rose on her arms; she'd stood in the fridge a lot longer than she realized. She picked up two square tiers that were meant for a small wedding cake and carried them out to the big stainless steel worktable.

As she assembled them and applied creamy white fondant that she had dressed up with a quilted look, she let the Zen of cake decorating take over. Away went thoughts of Jake, of her diet, of everything except the work in front of her as she piped borders and added strands of rhinestones and ribbons of thinly rolled fondant.

With tweezers she placed tiny pearlescent candies as the finishing touches on the cake then stepped back to check her work. Satisfied, she set it into the fridge and pulled out a tray of sugar flowers for another—white roses and purple asters.

"Sam? Lunch? We're ordering deli sandwiches," Jen said, holding the phone against her shoulder.

Lunch. She'd been determined to skip as many meals as possible this week but then Becky had lectured her on how unhealthy that was, not to mention counterproductive. "Just order me something as low-cal as possible."

By the time the delivery arrived, Sam felt her energy lagging and knew that the turkey breast on whole grain bread was a good answer. She'd taken one bite when her cell phone vibrated in her pocket.

"Samantha Jane, you never got back to me with the name of that hotel where you've got your aunt Bessie and uncle Chub staying. They need to call and be sure they're getting a king sized bed. You know how Chub can't sleep in one of those tiny, cramped up beds."

Leave it to her mother to micro-manage every detail of everyone's lives. Sam had put Kelly in charge of hotel reservations and felt sure she'd contacted everyone.

"I don't remember, off the top of my head, Mother. Didn't you get Kelly's email with the details?"

"Maybe so, but you know how I am with the computer. Your daddy probably read it and erased it."

"I'll ask Kelly to send it again." Sam scribbled herself a note at a desk that was already overloaded with little scraps of paper. She really had to get all this organized before leaving for two weeks.

"We'll all be there in three more days, honey. I just want to be sure everybody gets settled in all right. Now, your daddy and I are staying at that B&B of your friends? Is that right? And everyone else . . ."

Three days—yikes! Nina Rae's voice droned on, as she reiterated details Sam already knew. Sam ran a hand over her stomach, wondering if her waistline had gotten any smaller. She put the second half of her sandwich back in its container and closed the lid. No cookie for dessert either, she reminded herself.

". . . can't wait to see you in your beautiful dress. Samantha? You haven't said a word."

A vision of the zipper that wouldn't close flashed through Sam's head. "We're just really busy this week at the bakery, Mother."

"Oh my lord, that's the other thing. We've never seen your lovely little place of business. I can just hardly wait.

I bet it's just the most charming little place."

Sam glanced around at the sink full of dirty pans, the worktable loaded with unfinished cakes and the floor where Julio's last batch of batter had dribbled from the mixer to the oven. Charming. Sam picked up a damp towel.

"I really need to get back to work now, Mother. We'll see you in a few days."

She clicked off the call before Nina Rae could think of a new subject, some other bit of subtle pressure in the form of a chore Sam needed to do before The Day. She dropped the wet towel to the floor and pushed it with her foot until all the small batter drops were gone.

"Guys," she announced after calling Jen in from the sales room. "We've got to get this place in shape. Three days and the inspection we're getting will make the health department's visits seem like child's play. Okay, I'm exaggerating a little. But really, we do need to watch the little stuff. Clean up the messes when they happen, wipe down the counters. Jen, check the front window displays and the beverage bar and—"

"Sam. Got it. We have moms too," Jen said with a grin.

Even Julio smiled. Becky patted Sam's shoulder. "Why don't you tell us what we need to do for *your* cake, Sam. Your wedding is the most important thing happening this week. We can get the layers baked, make the flowers or whatever trims you have in mind . . . That's the main thing Mama Bear will want to see when she gets here, right?"

"Thanks. All of you. You're the best crew—"

The front door bells tinkled on their delicate chain and

Jen rushed out to attend to the new customer. A moment later the intercom buzzed. "Sam, there's a consultation out here."

Sam paused a beat. Jen had begun handling nearly all the consultations and orders recently. She set down her folder of sketches and headed for the sales room.

A young man sat at one of the tables, while Jen bustled to help three women who had apparently walked in at the same moment and were all talking at once. She sent Sam a grateful look.

"Vic Valentino," the young guy said, rising to shake Sam's hand. He was wiry thin with spiky hair that made him look as if he'd awakened in the middle of a tornado. "I need a spectacular cake. Of me."

"Okay . . ." Sam set her order pad on the table and sat down. "Tell me about the occasion."

Valentino perched on the edge of his chair, energy radiating out of him. "Well, I need to impress a judge."

Sam felt her eyebrows rise. "Court troubles?"

He laughed a little frantically. "Ha, ha, ha—no. Sorry I didn't explain that very well. A talent judge. I'm auditioning for *You're The Star.* You've probably heard of it. I heard that there are talent scouts in town and I need to beat the other contestants for the chance to audition. I read in *In The Know* magazine that somebody last year got onto one of those shows by wowing the judge with something he really liked. And *then* I heard that one of *these* judges really loves sweets. So, it's a no-brainer, right? I show up with a cake, they love the cake, they love me. Easy?"

"Well . . ."

Valentino continued. "So. Here's what I'm thinking. The cake is a stage, with these big spotlights and loads of glam. Stars, confetti, stuff like that. You could put some fireworks around the edges. And then there's a sculpture of me, and I'm in the middle of the stage holding a microphone, wowing them with my song. I composed it myself." He trilled out a few notes and the ladies at the counter spun around as if something were attacking them.

"Well, I won't sing it here. Can't give away all my moves ahead of time," Vic said. "I'll need the cake tomorrow."

She nearly objected to the tight deadline. The customer is always right, she reminded herself. As she sketched a rough idea of the design, Sam quickly calculated the number of extra hours this creation would involve: sculpting a lifelike figure, finding fireworks in September, finishing the whole thing in a day. She added the extra hours and tossed out a reasonable figure for the amount of work involved.

Vic Valentino winced. "Ouch. Any way you could, like, in the name of supporting an artist . . .?"

"I'm sorry, Mr. Valentino, we're super busy this week as it is. I normally charge an additional fifty percent for short notice like this, overtime for my staff, you know." She watched him argue the merits in his head.

"Okay, let's do it. This is my chance for my big break. And, heck, it's cheaper than traveling to L.A. to meet with these guys."

He pulled out a photograph that showed himself in a

sequined suit that would have made Liberace squint. He was standing on a stage in a karaoke bar and a man off to one side had an expression that said he'd kill for a set of earplugs.

Sam suppressed a laugh and wondered what the rest of the audience's reaction had been. Whatever it was, odds were that Vic Valentino had taken it as validation of his talent. He seemed like that kind of guy.

He began humming a few atonal notes and made his way over to the counter where Jen was now customer-less. With a casual arm atop the glass display the words "love is . . ." came out in a jarringly minor key.

She sent a heh-heh little smile toward him and then found something important to do in the other room.

"On custom cakes we require payment at the time the order is placed," Sam said to the man.

"Oh, yeah, right." At least he had to quit humming to answer her. He fished around in his pockets, pulling out cash of various denominations until he had come up with enough. Sam wrote a receipt and told him the cake would be ready after four p.m. the next day.

The moment the front door bells stopped moving, a giggle erupted from the back room. In the kitchen Sam found Jen and Becky practically holding their sides.

"Come on, girls, this is the man's drea—" A sputter of laughter came out. "Sorry. I can only imagine those judges' faces."

She took a deep breath and became businesslike. "It's a rush order. We need to get moving."

On that serious note Jen headed to the sales room

again and Sam began handing out assignments for the various elements on the Valentino cake.

Chapter 3

By five-thirty they'd made decent progress with the cake for the talent show auditioner. While Sam finished three other orders, Julio had baked and stacked layers to represent the stage, dirty-iced them and put them in the fridge to set up. Becky had the basics of a little figurine sculpted in white chocolate.

"Check the plastic bin on the top shelf," Sam told Becky. "I think we have some edible glitter that will work for the guy's sparkly suit. Now if I just knew where to come up with fireworks."

"I can get them," Julio said.

Sam didn't want to ask where he planned to shop since all but the smallest types were illegal and even those were usually unavailable after mid-summer. "Nothing that burns hot," she said. "We're working with icing here. Maybe just some sparklers."

He gave a pensive nod. "Got it."

Kelly peeked in at the back door. "Oh, hey. Didn't realize everyone was still here. Mom, are you coming by the house after work, or going straight out to Beau's?"

"I have an errand over on the plaza," Sam said. "After that I'll be at Beau's. Well, I guess I better get in the habit of calling the old house *your* place, since Beau's is now *ours*. Why?"

She'd bought a silver bracelet for her best friend Zoë, who was offering her bed and breakfast gratis for the ceremony, and the jeweler said she would have the engraving finished today. Sam glanced at the clock above the sink. She better get over there before the shop closed.

"Just deciding whether to pick up dinner for one or two," Kelly said. "It's feeling strange, making plans for myself only. Well, better go. One more client's coming by to pick up a dog, then I'm off."

Sam put her tools away and washed her hands, leaving Jen in charge of locking up.

The adobe buildings that ringed the plaza shone rose-gold in the late afternoon light. Sam lucked into a parking spot directly in front of the jewelry shop and the owner turned over the Closed sign after letting her inside.

Choosing a gift for Zoë hadn't been easy. Her friend dressed so casually, favoring loose skirts and embroidered tops, but when Sam had spotted the narrow silver bracelet with a flower motif lightly etched into it she knew it was Zoë.

Adelia Martinez, the jeweler, turned the piece around so Sam could see her words "Our friendship has bloomed, like a flower in a well-tended garden. With love from Sam."

"Thank you so much," Sam said. "It's just what I wanted for her."

For Kelly, as her maid of honor, Sam had chosen a different style bracelet—younger, stylish, with the added sparkle of a few tiny diamonds.

Adelia gave the bracelets a final polish with her cloth then wrapped them in satin bags within small boxes for each of the ladies.

Sam tucked the little prizes into her backpack and said goodbye. Out on the sidewalk she paused a minute to think. Wasn't there some other errand she'd intended to do before heading home? She glanced up and down the narrow street, looking for a memory jog, when she saw him again.

Walking right toward her came Jake Calendar. His appearance here seemed a little too coincidental until she remembered that he was staying at the La Fonda, just across the square from here. She crossed the sidewalk and stood by her van, half hoping he wouldn't notice her. No such luck.

"Sam, hello again," he said.

That's when she noticed the young woman with him. When Jake spoke the girl looped her arm through his. She was tall and slender with a model's face and posture, chin-length brown hair swept to one side and a pink dress that barely grazed the middle of her thighs.

"Evie, this is Samantha Sweet, the old friend from Alaska that I told you about. Sam, this is Evie Madsen."

An expression, something like relief, crossed Evie's face before she said hello. She raised her chin and pulled Jake closer, rubbing possessively against his arm. Three seconds passed as Sam tried to reconcile the picture of this man who was her age with this girl that could barely be out of college wrapped around him.

"Evie's with my crew. She's in charge of the audition venue."

Whatever that meant. She looked more in charge of keeping Jake's chest warm. A dozen wry comments came to mind but what Sam said was, "Nice to meet you."

Jake and the young appendage stepped aside for an older man to pass on the sidewalk.

"So you're already at that stage of things, auditioning people for your show?" Sam asked. "I may have met one of them at the bakery today."

Jake seemed distracted by a man who was staring at him from one of the benches in the center of the plaza. He turned away but the heavyset guy got up and walked toward them. He had a jowly, pockmarked face and dark eyes under ferocious eyebrows that went with the coarse blond hair on his head.

Jake saw him coming, muttered something that sounded like "damn cosart," and peeled away from Evie, meeting the man near the rear end of Sam's van. Sam watched as the rough-looking man said something under his breath and Jake responded with a shake of his head. The guy jabbed a finger at Jake's chest.

"You wanna watch out in little towns like this," he said clearly. "A guy can get real sick on a bad taco or somethin' like that."

He gave Jake a final, hard stare then turned and strode away across the plaza. Jake tugged at the hem of his jacket, straightening it. When he turned back toward Sam and Evie he had a rather forced smile on his face.

"So," he said. "We were actually just out to find a little cantina someone recommended, someplace around here. Sam, would you like to join us?"

Evie stepped on Jake's foot—not quite accidentally—then apologized half-heartedly.

"No, thanks. I'm getting on home to make dinner for Beau."

"Sam's engaged, Evie. The wedding is pretty soon, right?"

Sam edged toward the van, tired of being around Jake. She'd nearly reached her door when movement across the street caught her attention.

"Mom! Hey!" Kelly stood at the edge of the plaza, waving.

Before Sam could think of a way to stop her she'd skipped across the street, a small shopping bag dangling from her fingers. "Look what I found at Serendipity."

She reached into the bag, rummaging for something.

Sam glanced back at Jake.

"Oh, sorry," Kelly said. "I didn't realize you were talking to someone. I can show you this later."

She gave a small wiggle of the fingers in Jake and Evie's direction and headed back across the plaza where

Sam noticed Kelly's little red car was parked.

When Sam looked back toward Jake he was standing still as a statue. He knew.

"That's your daughter?" he said quietly.

"Yes. Well, I've got to get going." She opened the van's door. "Nice to meet you, Evie."

She slammed her door, started the engine and backed out of her spot before Jake could make a move. A small pickup truck blared its horn at her and she shoved the gearshift into Drive and got out of its way.

Jake knew. Well, what did she expect? One look at Kelly's curly brown hair and those aquamarine eyes that were identical to his—there was no way she could *not* be his kid. Had Kelly noticed?

There'd been no reaction but Sam couldn't take the chance. All Jake had to do was look up her number in the phone book. One call and Kelly would get a ton of questions she did not have answers to. Sam circled the block and headed for the house.

She caught up with Kelly's car a block from home and followed her into the driveway.

"It wasn't that important," Kelly said, holding up her little shopping bag as she got out of the car. "Just a new pair of earrings."

"There's something else. Something we should have talked about a long time ago."

Kelly's smile faded a touch and her forehead wrinkled.

"Let's go inside, maybe put the tea kettle on," Sam said.

"Mom? Is somebody sick or something?"

Sam draped an arm around Kelly's shoulders. "Nothing like that. C'mon, let's go in."

Kelly was already making the place her own, Sam noticed. Small touches, like a candle in the middle of the kitchen table, a mug Sam hadn't seen before. She felt a little pang.

She danced around the subject for a couple of minutes, filling the kettle with water, setting it on the burner. She'd had more than thirty years to prepare for this conversation but it all boiled down to the past fifteen minutes.

"Your father is in town," she began.

A crease formed between Kelly's eyebrows.

"I never thought I would see him again but here he is, shocking the hell out of me," Sam said.

"Did he come looking for me?"

Sam blew out a breath. "He actually contacted me, wanting money."

Kelly sank into one of the kitchen chairs. Sam adjusted the heat under the kettle.

"Kel, he never knew about you. We worked together in a temporary camp in Alaska. We were nineteen. Had a quick fling." She found it hard to look into Kelly's blue eyes. "When I discovered I was pregnant I left. Jake was—a free spirit, a guy who loved to move around, take a variety of jobs." Play around with a variety of women. She didn't say that.

"With a baby coming I knew I'd better settle somewhere. I couldn't go back to my parents in Texas; I never fit in there. I just bought a used Jeep, got in and started driving. Stopped when I came to Taos. This felt like home. It still does."

"You never told him about me? Ever?"

"No. I didn't."

The kettle let out a shriek. Sam turned off the burner and picked it up, suddenly not really wanting tea. She set it back down.

"I guess I got selfish, Kel. I didn't want to share you. Not with a man I barely knew, not with whatever extended family he might have. It was hard work, trying to support us both, but I loved our life together. Just us girls." They'd often used that phrase when Kelly was a kid. Just us girls.

"But what if he'd wanted to do the responsible thing and marry you and be a dad to me?"

He didn't. Sam would have bet on it. The picture of Jake with the young woman who was probably younger than Kelly popped into her head. She pressed her lips shut before a snide comment could come out.

"How could you *do* that to me, Mom? I never had a father, just because you felt a little *selfish* that day?"

"Kel, it wasn't—" It wasn't like that.

But Kelly had left the kitchen, stormed to her bedroom and closed the door a little too firmly.

Sam started after her but stopped short at the living room doorway. Pointing out that Kelly had never really asked questions about her father, nor had she expressed any particular regret about not having one—all that would be counterproductive at this moment. Give her some time. Sam picked up her pack and locked the back door behind her when she left.

At the ranch Beau was feeding the horses when she pulled up the long drive to the big log house. She left her pack on one of the porch chairs and walked toward the barn. The pinto nuzzled Beau's hand as he offered half an apple.

"Hey, darlin'," he said, turning toward her for a quick kiss. "Something wrong?"

She perked her mouth into a smile for him. "Kelly's upset with me. Long story."

Beau was another who deserved to know the whole truth. She'd told him about Jake, back when they began dating, but he didn't know the recent parts. She felt weary and not at all in the mood to get into it tonight.

"I put that chicken into the marinade when I got home," he said. "Anything else I can help you with?"

"Just keep being this wonderful," she said, hugging him around the middle. "I'll go in and finish dinner. Twenty minutes?"

* * *

Sam slept fitfully and was already wide awake when her alarm went off at four-thirty. By the time she arrived at the bakery she was feeling put-off because the scale had only showed a loss of two pounds and the way Kelly had slammed the door last night still echoed in her head. This couldn't go on. She would have to settle things with her daughter, and soon.

Two days until her mother, the ultimate lie detector, would be here. There was no way Sam and Kelly could be on bad terms during the family visit without everybody knowing what was going on. Sam checked the fridge to be sure Julio had baked the layers for her wedding cake, then set to work finalizing the audition cake for Vic Valentino.

It seemed clear now that either Jake or one of the others from his show would be the intended recipient. She pictured the way he'd wolfed down that cupcake in her shop. It was tempting to sneak some kind of bitter extract into the icing, but she discarded the thought. She didn't want him suing her—she preferred that he just get out of town soon.

The audition cake was ninety-percent done, only needing the fireworks and the figurine of Valentino, which Becky would finish this morning.

While Julio started baking the breakfast pastries for the display cases, Sam turned to making sugar flowers for her own cake. The color theme was autumn shades of orange, yellow and red so she started with tiger lilies, adding the tiny details that made them look as if they'd come straight from the florist. Realistic chrysanthemums took a lot of time but added great detail, so she made several of them too.

The intercom buzzed. "Sam? Mr. Calendar is here to see you."

God, Jake, could you possibly complicate my life any further?

She set the flowers to dry and wiped her hands on a towel. He stood at the beverage bar, helping himself to a cup of coffee.

"Jake, I told you I can't invest in your project."

He turned those blue eyes on her. "We need to talk about something else."

Oh boy. She turned to Jen. "I'll handle the front for a few minutes, if you can maybe check with Julio about getting some more scones out here?"

Jen raised an eyebrow but exited gracefully.

"Our last conversation ended a little too fast," he said. "I believe I'd just learned that you have a daughter. Or should I say, *we* do?"

"Lower your voice," she whispered. "No one knew about this. Including Kelly."

The light that sparked in his eyes worried her.

"You aren't going to blackmail me, Jake. I've told her."

"Good. I want to meet her."

It was all Sam could do not to glance toward the shop next door where Kelly would be at work right now.

"I want to clear that with her first. I'm not sure she wants to meet you."

His mouth opened. Closed again. "Fine. Today?"

Sam's foot tapped. Why not just get it over with now? Rip the bandage off all at once. "Let me give her a call. Wait here."

She walked into the kitchen and instructed Jen to watch the front again. Without a word Sam went out the back door and gave a quick tap at the back entrance to Puppy Chic then walked in.

Kelly was at the deep sink, sprayer in hand, rinsing suds off a small, shivering poodle.

"I need to talk to you," Sam said. "It's about that previous subject, the one that kept me awake half the night."

Judging by the circles under her eyes, Kelly must not

have rested all that well either.

"Mom, why is this all coming up now?" Her voice was chilly.

Deep breath. "Well, like I told you, he's in town. He—he's figured it out. About you."

"How?"

"Yesterday, on the plaza, the man who was standing there. That's Jake. I had hoped . . . well, I'd planned . . ."

What she'd hoped was that Jake would simply go away so that her life, and Kelly's, would continue as always before.

"When he saw you walking toward me, and when you called me mom . . . Well, you look a lot like him."

The breath seemed to go out of Kelly. She scrubbed at the poodle, her thoughts obviously churning.

"I look like him? How could I have not spotted that?"

"You had no reason to. But now he wants to meet you."

Kelly turned off the water and the dog clawed at the sides of the tub.

"He's at the bakery now. I can get you his number or set up a meeting for you . . . It's your call."

"I can come now," Kelly said. "Let me get Babycakes dried off and into a kennel. Riki should be back from the bank any second and I'll ask for an early lunch."

"Okay then. I'll tell him you'll come by the bakery in ten minutes. He doesn't need to know you work right here, at least until you know him better."

Kelly sent Sam that *don't be so overprotective look*, but at least there was a little smile attached.

Jake was flirting subtly with Jen when Sam walked back into the sales room. Jen sent a plea toward Sam and she shot him a look.

"Ten minutes. She'll meet you here, so go ahead and refill your coffee if you'd like. We've got work to do and I would appreciate it if you don't bother my employees."

Dirty old man, she fumed as she went back to the worktable.

She botched three flowers before convincing herself that she needed to concentrate on work. She could be as angry as she wanted with Jake, but later. When she heard the front door bells she went to the sales room to be sure Kelly and Jake got off on the right foot.

The two were studying each other but at least Jake's manner seemed respectful as he suggested they go for a walk. Kelly patted the front pocket of her jeans, her normal signal to Sam that she had her phone with her and would call if there was trouble. Sam felt herself giving a weak smile to the pair as they walked out.

Jen fidgeted behind the counter but managed to appear busy rather than pelting Sam with the questions she clearly wanted to ask.

Sam went back to the kitchen and spent the next ten minutes figuring out that her hands were far too shaky to form decent sugar flowers or pipe anything in icing. She ended up tinting fondant for a birthday cake order, kneading and pounding the paste color into it, imagining how it would feel to wad Jake Calendar into a lump of claylike dough and be done with him.

Chapter 4

Sam was draping the rolled pink fondant over a three layer red velvet birthday cake—her arms tired and her frustrations assuaged—when she heard the door bells tinkle. She smoothed the fondant and caught herself listening for Kelly's voice. *How long have they been gone? How long have I been working with one ear tuned to the other room?*

She picked up a knife to trim away the excess fondant and realized that the voice she was hearing out front was Beau's. A glance at the clock told her it was nearly twelve and she remembered he had mentioned getting together for lunch. She turned the cake project over to Becky and washed her hands.

"Hey you," she said when she walked into the sales room.

"I come bearing gifts," he said. "Well, actually, it's just your mail. I had to stop by the post office anyway." The small stack appeared to be mainly catalogs, with a couple of letter-sized envelopes included. One of them was heavy white paper with a very business-like return address imprinted on it. She squeezed it, testing the thickness of the contents.

"What's this?" she muttered, half to herself.

She set the other mail on a table and ripped open the interesting one. Two sheets of paper came out. The letterhead indicated that it came from a legal firm in New York and she scanned to the bottom to see that it was signed by a Clinton Hardgate, Esq.

Dear Ms. Sweet,

I am writing to inform you—

The door opened and Sam glanced up to see Jake Calendar. Kelly was walking toward Puppy Chic and Sam couldn't read anything in her daughter's step to let her know how the visit had gone. Jake didn't appear to notice Beau standing by the display case; he stood beside Sam and gave a curious stare at the letter in her hand. She folded it, stuffed it back in the envelope and jammed the envelope between two catalogs.

"I'm so proud of her," Jake said in the way two parents might reminisce at their kid's graduation.

Like you had anything to do with that. She noticed that Beau was studying Jake. She called him over and introduced them—first names, no details about Jake.

"Beau is my fiancé," she said with pride.

He slipped an arm over her shoulders. Jake took the

hint, made a few polite noises and left. When Sam looked up at Beau she saw the questions in his eyes.

"Lunch?" she asked.

They walked out to his cruiser and he suggested a place they liked, where it would be quiet enough to talk but busy enough to keep the conversation private.

"So that was Jake."

"That was Jake."

"He in town long?"

"I certainly hope not." Sam launched into the explanation of how Jake had showed up out of the blue and immediately asked her for money, how he'd figured out about Kelly and insisted on a meeting.

"Sounds like it was a little rough between you and Kelly. No wonder you slept like a kitten on uppers last night."

"Was I tossing around that badly?"

He gave a rueful smile. "Yeah. So, now that he's met Kelly, what next?"

"You saw what just happened. She went back to work, he made it sound all chummy. I guess I'll have to get her version of it to see how she handled it."

"How are *you* handling it? Is there still a spark?"

"Beau! No. *No.*" There had been a huge spark thirty-plus years ago but she truly felt nothing but irritation for Jake now.

Beau edged a glance her way, reading her face.

"There isn't. No more than you felt for Felicia Black when she showed up in your life awhile back. At least Jake isn't making romantic overtures toward me."

A muscle in his jaw twitched but he didn't interrupt.

"He's got a girlfriend with him. She's probably younger than Kelly. It's disgusting to see a middle-aged man act that way."

He let her vent and by the time they'd pulled into a parking slot along Bent Street both had relaxed. Sam rummaged through the pile of mail in her lap, pulled out the letter she'd only begun to read and carried it with her. They were shown to a table outdoors under an elm tree and they placed orders for their favorites without even looking at the menus.

"So, what's in the letter?" Beau asked.

Sam settled back in her chair and opened it.

Dear Ms. Sweet,
I am writing to inform you of the death of your great-uncle, Terrance O'Shaughnessy of Galway, Ireland.

She felt her brows pull together.

As Mr. O'Shaughnessy's personal representatives, our firm is charged with disposition of his assets and I am pleased to inform you that there is a bequest in your name. Please call me at the number above, as I need details to finalize the enclosed airline reservations for yourself and your companion.
My condolences at your loss.
Yours sincerely,
Clinton Hardgate

"Ireland?" Sam passed the page over to Beau and took a look at the other sheet. It appeared to be a printout for two airline tickets, first class, from New York City to Shannon, Ireland.

"Who's this uncle?" Beau asked.

"Good question. I've never heard of him." Sam studied the two pages again. "I don't know . . . this could be some kind of scam. You know, send us your bank account number and we'll give you this *free* thing."

Beau looked at the description of the plane tickets. "It's dated the twenty-second. That would be the day after our wedding. Could someone know about that?"

"I don't see how. My family from Texas, those of us in the wedding party, our closest friends—they're the only ones who know the date. We didn't even put an announcement in the newspaper."

Their sandwiches arrived and Sam slid the pages back into the envelope.

"I'll do a little background research when I get back to the office," Beau said. "We can find out if this law firm is legit and maybe see if there really is a Terrance O'Shaughnessy in Galway."

"I imagine there could be dozens of O'Shaughnessys," Sam pointed out. "I'll ask my folks too. They'll be here this afternoon."

She felt a ripple of anticipation. She tended to become irritated with her mother's intrusive questions when they spoke on the phone, but her dad had always been a calming influence and it would be good to see him, to get a better feel for his health and state of mind. And then there were the aunts and uncles, most of whom she hadn't seen in at least twenty years. It would be nice to turn the bakery over to the employees and simply relax with family for a few days.

"It's not like we couldn't do it," Beau was saying.

"Go to Ireland? Well, we do have passports. We've arranged time off work. And it sounds a lot more intriguing than our driving trip. I mean, the Grand Canyon will still be there next year."

Beau glanced at the envelope. "Before we get too excited, we better find out if there's any way this could be legit."

"Take it with you so you'll have all the information. Let me know what you find."

"Okay. But don't be surprised if there's some scam artist behind it all."

They paid their tab and Beau dropped Sam off at the bakery. She walked in to find that Becky had stepped up to finish the sugar flowers for Sam's cake. She approved the results and they set the flowers aside to dry, getting back to the daily bakery orders and finalizing the audition cake for Vic Valentino with the small fireworks Julio had supplied. Sam didn't ask—as the sheriff's fiancée she didn't really want to know—where he'd gotten them.

Although Sam had told the wannabe singer to come after four o'clock Jen announced his arrival at a little after three. Sam carried the cake out front and watched with amusement as he focused on the skinny little figurine of himself with his gelled hair and spangled suit.

"I *love* it!" He pointed to the spotlights and the microphone. "It's so *me!*"

She asked Jen to assemble a box for it.

"That producer is going to be blown away," Valentino

said. "I'll get on *You're The Star* for sure."

The show whose producers were still scrambling for funding. Even if Vic had the talent to make it to national television she had serious doubts that this particular show would ever see airtime. She didn't have the heart to say it to the young man though. She watched him place the cake into the back seat of a rundown Chevy and back out of his parking slot. Good luck, she thought as she saw the old beater drive away.

Her phone rang as she headed back to the kitchen.

"Mom, I meant to tell you earlier, but after we talked this morning Jake invited me to dinner. He wants a little more time together. I told him I would meet him in front of his hotel." Kelly's voice still seemed a little cool.

Sam gave herself a couple of beats before she spoke. "Your grandparents are coming in this afternoon. They'll want to see you."

"I know, and I'd forgotten about that when I said yes to Jake. But he said he's probably leaving town in the next couple days. And I'll have time with them all the way through the weekend."

"Whatever you think," Sam said. "By the way, they don't know much about Jake. Until I know whether he's going to become a permanent factor in your life, I'd rather not bring up the subject with them. Okay?"

She sighed as she hung up. Her own apprehensions about Jake Calendar were irrelevant right now. Kelly would do whatever she wanted to. Sam could only hope she would keep her head straight and not be rude to the rest of the family.

No sooner had that thought emerged than Sam heard a familiar voice.

"Oh. My. *Lord*. This place is just so *cute*!" Nina Rae Sweet had a voice that could fill an arena whenever she got excited.

Sam quickly scanned the kitchen, happy to see that Becky's stack of orders was under control. She'd nearly finished a traditional birthday cake for one of their older customers; there was only a child's cake to finish today, a carousel with bright striping and fat ducks instead of horses. Julio had just placed baking sheets with six dozen cookies into the oven for the late-afternoon crowd and was in the process of washing up the mixing bowls and utensils.

"Showtime, guys," she murmured before turning to walk out to the front.

"Samantha Jane! I just *love* it!" Nina Rae rushed forward, her rail-thin arms outstretched. How her mother managed to stay so slender Sam had never figured out. As always, her chin-length hair had been freshly done in her favorite shade of mink and the precise waves stayed exactly in place. Her makeup never changed except for her eye shadow color, which always went with the outfit of the day, this time a subtle beige pantsuit.

"You've got the *purple* . . . and look how good those pastries . . . well. Oh, and you know the *first* thing we spotted? Those cakes you have in that front window display. They're just absolutely—gorgeous."

She turned to Jen. "You know, I can't believe Samantha opened her shop almost a year ago and we hadn't gotten out here to see it."

Jen started to reply but Nina Rae was looking in another direction.

"And *look* at these cute little tables and chairs! A person just couldn't *help* coming in off the street for a nice cup of coffee and a *pastry*, now could they?"

Jen closed her mouth and nodded.

"Samantha, you look so *good*, honey. Beau has been good for you. I can just tell it."

Sam started to answer but Nina Rae was onto something else already.

"Well, do I get to see the kitchen? Unless it's, you know, out of bounds or something. But you know, I'd *love* to see your work space."

Sam pointed toward the curtain across the doorway that divided the two rooms.

"How are you, Daddy?" she asked as her mother breezed past and she got the chance to hug her father. He looked a little thinner than last January when she and Beau had made a quick trip to Texas to see them.

"I'm fine, Sammy. Life is treatin' me good."

When he'd first retired from his corporate accounting position, Howard Sweet was a little at loose ends, Sam recalled. But he'd quickly taken up golf and fishing, two pastimes that kept him out of the house and on the go quite a bit. And when indoors, he usually had some type of sports program on the TV. She had to admit that he seemed content.

An exclamation from the back told Sam that her mother had spotted the birthday cake that Becky was finishing. She signaled for Jen to join them so she could handle all the introductions at once. Once she knew all their names, it seemed Nina Rae had questions for everyone.

Sam spent a moment neatening the papers on her desk then called Kelly to see if she was free to pop over and say hello. When she arrived, Kelly greeted her grandparents with hugs.

"I want to see *your* cake, Samantha, and of course your dress," Nina Rae said. "Hasn't your mama done just a fantastic job with the bakery, Kelly?"

"The cake isn't finished, Mother," Sam said, saving Kelly from having her cheeks pinched.

Nina Rae turned back to Sam. "Well, it wouldn't be, not yet, but do you have a design done up?"

Sam showed the sketches and the sugar flowers she and Becky had made earlier. Even that bit of information seemed to pacify Nina Rae and distract her from the subject of the dress. There was no way Sam intended to model it at this point. She made a mental note to go by Kelly's and try it on again to see if she'd made any progress with her weight loss.

"Now, Aunt Bessie and Uncle Chub will be here by suppertime," Nina Rae said once they'd finished a quick tour of the kitchen. "They flew from Oklahoma City into Albuquerque and they are meeting up with Lub, who's going to drive them up here."

She turned to Jen. "Chub doesn't drive out on the highway much anymore."

Sam had already given Beau and her staff a little

primer on the odd nicknames in her family. Chub was Charles, Howard's brother. How he'd gotten the name Chub was a little unclear, as he'd never been the least bit overweight. Their son Lester had immediately been stuck with Lub, which might have happened because as a kid he *was* rather pudgy but the name Chub had already been assigned to his father.

"There's something about the South," Sam had warned her crew. "Your childhood nickname stays with you forever. Anyplace else they would have ditched those names well before high school, but not in Texas. There are grown men who think nothing of being called Bubba or Toots or Dusty."

"So what was your childhood nickname?" Becky had teased.

She changed the subject.

"Now do Bessie and Chub know which hotel they're at?" Nina Rae asked.

Sam assured her that everyone had received complete instructions. Inside, she had qualms about the fact that they were at the La Fonda, the same place Jake was staying, but since none knew each other and Kelly had been warned about spilling the secret, Sam could only hope everything would be all right until Jake left town.

"Tonight we're meeting for dinner at a place Beau and I really like. Everyone has directions to get there," she said. "And right now I'm going to take you over to Zoë's bed and breakfast. Daddy, you can follow me over there, then I'll get back to work while y'all get settled in." *Oh, god. Ten minutes with them and I'm speaking Texan again.*

Sam led the way with her bakery van covered in the decal motif that made it look like a big box of pastries. Zoë was waiting for them and showed the parents to her best room. She suggested that they freshen up if they'd like and then she would serve tea and show them around the place, including the garden where the ceremony would take place.

"How do you manage to anticipate her questions before she even asks?" Sam said as she and Zoë parted at the back door.

Zoë tugged at the tunic top she wore over a flowered broomstick skirt. "I've hosted many moms of many brides. I had a little clue what she would be after."

"Daddy might want a nap before dinner," Sam suggested, "so if you could keep Mother entertained for a little while . . ."

"No problem. Before she knows it she'll be helping me make flower arrangements for the tables."

Sam hugged Zoë and thanked her. As she drove away she let out a long breath. One hour with her parents and she was tired already.

Chapter 5

A deep azure sky set off the gold cottonwood leaves, rendered more brilliant by the low afternoon sun. Sam headed toward her old house—Kelly's now—almost on automatic pilot, but feeling the urgency of her mission. She hit the speed dial for Rupert.

"Are you busy?"

"Sweetie, I just typed 'The End' on my newest and I'm ready to chill."

"I'm on my way to the house. I need to find out if all my half-eaten meals and calorie consciousness helped. Can you come by and do another zipper check?"

"I'll be there in ten."

Sam let herself in and went straight to her old bedroom where the dress hung on a padded hanger from the top of the closet door. She ran her fingers appreciatively over the beautiful fabric and envisioned herself stately and slender in it. She got the stately part down fine but slender still eluded her. On top of her dresser the carved wooden box containing her jewelry sat like a dull lump. If things had feelings Sam would swear it was miffed that she hadn't yet moved it to her new home.

She walked over and ran her hand across the top of the quilt-patterned carving. The wood immediately lightened and warmed slightly to her touch. A knock at the back door startled her and she turned away.

"Yoo-hoo? Sam?" came Rupert's voice.

"In here," she called out. "Give me just a minute." She pulled off her bakery attire and stepped into the silk and lace confection. Easing the cap sleeves up to her shoulders, she called Rupert to join her.

"What do you think?" she asked after he'd pulled the zipper up as far as it would go.

"A good foundation garment and ten more pounds, and this thing will *glide* up," he said.

"Ten pounds? I've got less than three days and we're going out to dinner tonight."

"There's still that spa in Santa Fe."

"No time for that, Rupe. I'm doing good to stay above water as it is. Kelly still needs more training on the houses, my parents are here, the rest of the family are arriving all day tomorrow, and my cake is less than half ready."

"Minnie Rodrigues is good with alterations, but she'll need some time."

Sam closed her eyes, debating and picturing herself running at full speed for the next three days. "I think I can manage the ten pounds."

Rupert unzipped the dress. "I know you will." He grazed a kiss on her cheek and told her to call him if she changed her mind. He offered to put Minnie on alert in case it was a last-minute thing. Wishing Sam luck with her mother, he left.

Sam gazed at the wooden box again, that mysterious little artifact that had been placed in her hands by a supposed *bruja*, the old woman on her deathbed telling Sam that the box would help her in many ways. *Including giving me the serenity to cope with all my relatives?*

She picked it up and hugged it to the bodice of her wedding dress, imagining the remainder of the week and this weekend going without a hitch. As the wood warmed Sam found herself calming. Everything would work out fine.

She took a deep breath and set the box on the bed, slipped out of the dress and put her clothes back on. It seemed that her slacks buttoned more easily than they had this morning. She stared at the box.

Nah. No way.

Out in the van Sam set the wooden box on the passenger seat and thought of the attorney in New York. What was she going to do about that?

Kelly's little red car pulled in beside the van and Sam powered down the window long enough to tell her daughter to have a good time. At dinner. With Jake. Although Sam felt a momentary pang at sharing with the newly discovered father, she put a smile on and hoped Kelly didn't see her misgivings.

She arrived home to find Beau's Explorer parked beside the house but no sign of him or the dogs outside. The barn was closed up and the horses were grazing contentedly at the far end of the pasture. She gathered her belongings and went inside to be greeted enthusiastically by the border collie.

"Hey, Nellie, how's the girl?" Sam ruffled the dog's coat and noticed that Beau had left the attorney's letter on an end table. She headed upstairs to put the wooden box in a safe spot and change her clothes.

At the head of the stairs she caught the scent of soap and a steamy shower. Beau emerged as Sam was studying her side of the closet for something to wear to dinner.

"I got some background on that attorney, the one who sent the letter," Beau said, toweling his hair dry. "The firm is legit and Clinton Hardgate has been licensed to practice in New York since 1968. They specialize in estates and wills, and have agreements in place with other firms around the world where estate matters involve parties in different countries. I was able to get that much from public records. When I spoke to Hardgate himself he confirmed that they work with a legal firm in Galway, but he will only give the particulars of your inheritance directly to you. Which makes sense. I'm glad to see he's careful about such things. All you have to do is call him. Said he'll be at his office until eight o'clock tonight, or all day tomorrow."

Sam thought about all of it while she showered and

pulled on a dressy pair of slacks and one of her favorite blouses. It was still only five-thirty, so she dialed the number on the letterhead and pressed the extension that Beau had obtained directly to Hardgate's line.

"I was shocked to get your letter," she said after introducing herself. "I had no idea there was an uncle in Ireland."

"Well, if you are the Samantha Sweet who was born in Cottonville, Texas, Terrance O'Shaughnessy was your uncle. You've verified the other information I have in my files, and based on that I'm authorized to cover airfare and hotel for yourself and a companion. Of course, you'll have to present yourself at the offices of Ryan and O'Connor in Galway and show your identification, etcetera, before you'll receive anything more than the travel expenses."

"Do you have any idea what the inheritance consists of? Not that it matters a lot, but I'm puzzled. Why me?"

"Apparently, Mr. O'Shaughnessy was married but had no children. He planned to divide his estate among the children of his nieces, choosing one from each branch of the family. Unfortunately, your aunt, Lily Bowlin, never had children. I'm not clear on how the choice was made, but now it appears you are the sole heir."

This news probably wouldn't go over well with her sister, Rayleen. Sam decided not to mention the possibility of money until she knew more about the whole situation. For all she knew the inheritance might consist of something equivalent to the wooden box she'd gotten from Bertha Martinez, a gift that Rayleen would find useless and, in her words, tacky.

Hardgate continued: "The airline reservation is flexible. I simply chose a date randomly, but you can change that. I only need your passport numbers and full names. And I will contact Ryan and O'Connor, who will finalize all other arrangements in Galway for you."

Sam realized they were running late to pick up her parents and promised to get back to him with the information within a day.

"You're right about the letter being genuine," she said to Beau as they walked out to his Explorer. "So, what do you think about changing our honeymoon plans and going to Ireland instead? Air and hotel all paid. And who knows what this mysterious inheritance might be?"

"Maybe a big fat bank account, so we can both retire early." He chuckled as he turned onto the road.

"Maybe a smaller bank account, but we could still do some traveling?"

"Maybe a title—do they have dukes and earls and such in Ireland?"

"Maybe a castle!" She let her eyes light up at the outlandish thought.

"Most likely it's a vacation to Ireland and some kind of memento like a lucky shamrock."

"Which wouldn't be so bad either," she said. "Just FYI, let's don't say anything about any inheritance until we find out what's involved. Hardgate said something about this uncle making a choice from among all the nieces on Mother's side of the family. I'd hate to think about there being a big catfight over the leaves of some lucky clover."

Beau took a shortcut that avoided the tourist traffic

around the plaza and pulled into the front parking area at Zoë and Darryl's place. They went inside, where Sam found her mother wearing a fresh outfit, a purple dress in some crepe-like fabric. Her dad was chatting with Darryl about the price of two-by-four lumber these days.

"Are you sure you guys won't join us all for dinner?" Sam asked Zoë, even though she already knew the answer before Zoë shook her head.

Nina Rae piped up: "We've spoken with Bessie and Chub, and they're going to meet us at this place. I warned them it isn't going to be Tex-Mex."

Beau laughed. "Not around here, it won't. I hope everyone is up for authentic New Mexican food."

He placed a gentlemanly hand on Nina Rae's elbow and the group headed for his vehicle. At the restaurant Bessie and Chub were standing in the vestibule of the converted Spanish hacienda, staring at the paintings and sculpture by local artists.

Bessie, a quintessentially well-mannered Southern woman with a petite build, short blond hair and a sparkle in her blue eyes, greeted Sam with a warm hug. Her husband, Charles, looked more like Sam's dad every year. Although he'd shed the nickname Chub in the outside world, the family had never quite dropped it. He stood quietly aside until the women finished their exclamations and Sam finally introduced him to Beau. By the ready smile that lit Beau's face, she knew these two would hit it off well.

"So, is this all of our group for tonight?" Howard asked.

"I bet I've said this a *hundred* times, Howard," said Nina Rae. "Lily and Buster and Wilhelmina will be coming in tomorrow. Rayleen and Joe Bob and the kids can't get away until Thursday night but they're driving straight on through and will get here Friday by noon." She turned to the rest of the group. "Ya'll aren't going to believe how those *grandsons* of mine have *grown*."

Luis, their favorite waiter at Casa Benito, escorted them through a courtyard where petunias still bloomed in profuse clumps of purple and pink and water trickled down a stack of artfully arranged rocks into a small fishpond. He showed them to a table in a private room with windows overlooking the garden. Once assured that everyone was seated he took orders for beverages. Nina Rae, seated across from Sam, reiterated her warning—a little under her breath—that the food wouldn't be their usual Texas versions of Mexican food. Sam noticed that even Bessie nodded a little impatiently.

"Mother," Sam said after their food orders had been taken and the others had started a conversation at their end of the long table, "I just heard that we had an uncle in Ireland. I never knew that."

"Well, I'm sure I'd told you about him. Terrance. Mother used to call him Uncle Terry when Lily and I were children. I remember him visiting us at the farm once. Gosh, I must have been only about seven or so. Lily was a baby, I'm sure of it."

"So you never really knew him, personally?"

"When we were just little bitty, they used to send us little Irish gifts at Christmas. He and Aunt Maggie." Nina

Rae rolled her eyes upward, thinking. "Maggie must have passed on more than twenty-five years ago. Uncle Terry was actually younger than she was, I believe."

"But you hadn't heard from him in recent years?" Sam asked.

Nina Rae shook her head. "Not a word."

Their food arrived and the conversation turned to tastes and comparisons. Sam found herself intrigued by this unknown uncle and what his life must have been like. She'd ordered a simple bowl of chile stew and took her time spooning it up, trying to make herself feel full by imagining how her dress needed to fit. By the time the sopapillas with honey arrived for dessert, she managed to pass the basket along to Beau without feeling tempted by them. *Almost* not tempted.

When she noticed her father stifling a yawn she suggested that they make it an early evening. No one disagreed, and they said goodnight to Bessie and Chub outside in the parking lot, then took her parents back to Zoë's.

"Okay, we need to find our passports so I can call Clinton Hardgate back first thing in the morning," she said when she and Beau got home. "If he can still get flights for us the day after the wedding, I say let's do it."

Beau found his documents easily enough in the very organized desk he kept in one corner of the great room. Sam spent nearly an hour rummaging through the boxes that she hadn't quite unpacked yet, finally locating hers in a shoebox full of important papers that was labeled 'White Sandals.'

"Just think—Ireland—the Emerald Isle. I picture white sheep grazing, stone walls and adorable little cottages," she told Beau as she placed the passports and letter on the kitchen counter where she would see them in the morning. "I'm really getting excited about this trip."

He pulled her close and rested his chin on top of her head. "Me too. But I'm more excited that we're starting our life together."

"We're good as a pair, aren't we?"

"We are that."

He kissed her hair, then her temple, and was aiming for her mouth when her phone buzzed.

"Woo! Is that a vibrator in your pocket or are you just happy—"

She laughed and checked the readout. Kelly. "I better see what's going on."

"I'll meet you in the bedroom," he said, giving her shoulders a gentle squeeze.

"Kel? Everything okay?"

"Oh, god, Mom. What a disaster."

Sam's heart skipped. "What happened? Did he hurt you?"

"No, no. I'm fine." A huge sigh. "It's just . . . Are all men such jerks?" At least her tone was no longer aloof.

"Kel, you know they aren't." Sam settled into a corner of the sofa. "You want to talk about it?"

Another sigh.

"Grab yourself a Coke or something and tell me. Well, if you want to."

Kelly mumbled something and then Sam heard the

metal tab on a soda can.

"First off, it was really a little shocking to meet his date. Mom, she was younger than me!"

Evie. Sam remembered the slender woman in her tight pink dress.

"She reminded me so much of all those girls out in L.A. Gorgeous but just about intelligent enough to string one sentence together. She hung on him as if I were competition. Ick! I couldn't believe it."

"Well, to be fair, he'd already brought her on the trip before he knew anything about you," Sam offered.

"It doesn't matter. He's fifty-something, she's about twenty. It's gross."

"Yeah, I agree."

"Then he was just rude, Mom. Incredibly rude. This young guy showed up outside the hotel as we were leaving. He was sort of a nutcase himself, really. Dressed in some sparkly suit and he had a cake. It was a beautiful cake, and you probably made it because it was nothing he would have found on the shelf somewhere. So, okay, he gets Jake's attention and hands him the cake, then he starts jumping around and dashing all over the place while singing—and I use that word *very* loosely—singing some horrendous song.

"I found out later that Jake is with some kind of talent show for TV and figured out that this guy wanted a sort of advance audition, even though that definitely would not be the way to impress a judge, okay? But Jake didn't even have the grace to be kind about rejecting the guy. He screamed at him to shut up, then he threw the cake down on the ground. I mean, people were stopping on the sidewalk—cars squealed their brakes. I felt humiliated. I can only imagine what that poor guy felt like." She took a deep breath. "It was awful."

"So, did you go to dinner after all that?"

"Jake linked arms with me and *Evie* and we went back inside the hotel and went to the restaurant there."

"So it got better after that?"

"No! God, that was the thing. Between him bragging about all the people in Hollywood he knows and Evie practically crawling in his lap, I took about three bites of the appetizer and half my wine and said I wasn't feeling very well. I got out. Was that awful of me?"

"Leaving behind half a glass of expensive wine? What were you thinking?"

Kelly started to laugh. "Leave it to Mom to put things in perspective. I'm better now. I came home and made myself a peanut butter sandwich. I'm having a shower and then I'm giving up on reality TV forever."

"Oh, no, not that! How will you live without it?" Sam dramatized her voice until Kelly began to howl.

"Okay, not *every* show. But I'll tell you, you won't catch me watching *You're The Star*. Never, ever, ever!"

What was it with Jake Calendar? Charming one minute and losing his temper the next. If he couldn't go out of his way just a little bit to make a special evening for his daughter, then neither of them would miss him in their lives.

"Join us tomorrow night for steaks out here at the house. Most of the aunts and some of the cousins will

be here. And, I'll have an odd surprise to tell you about.
Beau and I have changed our honeymoon plans."

Chapter 6

Sam woke up well before her alarm went off, a vague dream of a small town in Ireland floating through her head after she and Beau had talked about the trip late into the night. She wondered how early Clinton Hardgate would arrive in his office.

Dressing in her usual bakery attire—black slacks and a spotless white baker's jacket with the store logo embroidered in purple—she left Beau peacefully sleeping and made her way downstairs. She started the coffee maker for him, gathered the passports and the lawyer's letter, and headed toward town.

Julio's Harley sat outside the back door to Sweet's Sweets and the scent of cinnamon rolls greeted her when she walked in.

"You really got in early," she said as she set the papers on her desk and reviewed the list of orders for the day.

He nodded, murmured something about hoping to get away early, and turned back to the mixer where muffin batter was getting a good stir.

Sam pulled the layers for her own cake out of the fridge, along with tinted fondant in creamy ivory and sunshine yellow. The design called for four tiers, alternating between pale tones and vivid autumn ones. The ivory fondant would cover the largest, bottom tier with wide burnt-orange hatbox stripes to add a touch of class.

The next tier would be entirely covered in the dark orange, with scrolls of old-fashioned piping for a slightly Victorian flair. The third tier was to be a fantasy of sunny yellow with a garland of beads and baubles in autumn colors, and the fourth would cap it with a repeat of the striping—narrow pinstripes this time—and a cascade of autumn sugar flowers and burgundy ribbons.

It was way too much cake for the small gathering of fewer than twenty-five guests, but this was something Sam had dreamed of for a long time and she wasn't going to skimp with a tiny cake.

She ran the fondant through the rolling machine and began placing and trimming it to fit the tiers. By the time Becky arrived, Sam had inserted the support dowels and together they began to stack tiers.

"We'll let this set up until tomorrow," she told her assistant, "then we can do final assembly and still have a day to spare."

"Are you getting excited?" Becky asked.

"I am. And wait 'til you hear the best part," Sam said. "Our honeymoon plans have changed. Which reminds me, I need to make a call to the east coast and I'll bet this would be a good time."

They moved the cake into the walk-in fridge and Sam pointed out a couple of projects that Becky should get done soon, then she gathered the information she needed and placed the call to the attorney.

"All set," she told Beau on the phone a little later. "Sunday morning we're on a flight out of Albuquerque to New York, then it's direct to Shannon and we'll be met by our own car and driver for the ride to Galway."

"I'm liking this being married to an heiress," he said. "First class travel *and* limo service. I could get used to that."

She laughed. "Well, don't get used to it too soon. We still have no idea how far this will go."

"Yeah, it'll probably end up being some huge, drafty old castle."

"With heating bills that will bankrupt us."

She heard his intercom buzz in the background and they ended the call. She'd no sooner stuck her phone in her pocket than Kelly peeked in at the back door.

"Things are pretty slow next door this morning," she said. "Want to use the time to finish going over those properties?"

Sam glanced around her. Julio and Becky had things well under control and she couldn't imagine things would get any less busy in the next two days.

"Perfect," she said. "Let me grab my file."

She pulled open a desk drawer and picked out the folder listing her current USDA properties. Inside were details Kelly might need to know: contact information for Delbert Crow, her contracting officer, who'd already been notified that Sam would be away for two weeks; addresses of the three houses under her care; a procedures checklist Sam had written up, one she had planned to keep brief but which had grown each time she thought of some new thing to add.

"You drive," she said to Kelly. "I'm leaving you the keys to my truck so you have all the tools and yard maintenance gear. I doubt you'll have to take on a new property. Delbert knows that I'm leaving town and there's usually nothing so urgent that it can't wait a little while. So, all you have to do is go by each of these three places about once a week and check them over."

Two of the houses on the list still needed to be winterized and they decided to start with the one farther away, a small house on a few acres of land south of town. Sam reviewed the procedures and let Kelly do the work, pointing out certain notes on her checklist.

"You doing better after that little fiasco last night?" Sam asked as they walked through the empty house, checking windows and doors.

"Yeah. Sorry I vented on you."

"Has he tried to contact you again?"

"He called once, right after I left the restaurant. Said he was sorry if he embarrassed me with the cake incident. He sounded sincere about that."

Sorry for embarrassing Kelly, not sorry for his own actions. That reminded her of the old Jake.

"Did he suggest getting together again?"

"Vaguely. But I don't know. It wasn't just the fact that he lost patience with the guy who tried to audition. He probably gets that kind of thing a lot. And the guy really had no chance of getting onto the show . . ."

"But?"

"Well, it was just the way he did it. Two minutes earlier he'd been all smiles and politeness. I don't trust people whose moods change that fast. You know? It's like he's super polite when there's something in it for him, but to somebody unimportant he just blows them off."

Jake had always been a charmer. Sam knew it so well, the way he'd lured her into his bed, even though there'd been no talk of making plans or permanency about the relationship. Of course she had herself to blame for that too.

"If he wants to try again for a meal, I might go," Kelly said. "I don't know . . . there's the whole young-Evie thing too. I just . . . I haven't seen much to admire about him, Mom. I should probably give him more of a chance, but I really don't get the feeling I'm going to like him much."

"Well, you'll figure it out." Down inside, her heart was doing little leaps of joy. The last thing she needed was Jake Calendar hanging around now that he knew where to find them.

Kelly pointed to a window latch that didn't seem secure and asked whether she should get it repaired. Sam gave it a tug and was able to turn the latch to a better position. They finished checking the place and left.

By the time they reached the second property, a condo near the movie theater, Kelly had the steps down pat for getting into the lockboxes and remembering to sign in on the sheet that documented the work they were doing. Thirty minutes per house, per week should be adequate considering there weren't lawns to mow or shrubs to trim this time of year. They headed back to the middle of town.

"Okay, now that everything is ready for cold weather," Sam said, "you should be able to handle it from here. Drop me back at the bakery and go on to the Bowen Road place that we worked on together the other day. Check it over. Pay special attention for any sign of mice. They love to come indoors once the seasons change. Go ahead and scatter some poison around. There's a can of Ratzout in that plastic supply bin in the back. Call me if you run into any snags but I want you to get a feel for being there and making all the decisions on your own."

"*Mom*, I'm not three."

Sam glanced at her daughter. "Sorry. I— I sounded just like my mother, didn't I?"

"Pretty much." Kelly's eyes twinkled. "Actually, a lot."

"Oh, god. *So* sorry!"

Kelly pulled up in front of Sweet's Sweets. "It's okay. Someday I'll probably do that to my own kid."

"Plan to come to dinner out at Beau's tonight. The rest of the aunts, uncles and cousins should be coming in today and we're going to grill steaks and give everyone an informal place to visit all they want. And you *know* they all want to see you." She got out of the truck and patted the door as Kelly drove away.

Sam walked into her shop where Jen had two customers and the phone was ringing. Within moments Sam became caught up and the rest of the afternoon went by in a blur. At some point Beau called to say that he would pick up the steaks if she didn't have time. Her mother called to let her know that Uncle Buster, Aunt Lily and her cousin Wilhelmina had arrived in town.

Nina Rae, Bessie and Lily planned to make the rounds of the art galleries. Since that would bring them within two blocks of her shop, Sam wasn't surprised when the ladies stopped in.

"Isn't it the most *darling* little place?" Nina Rae said.

Sam gave her aunt Lily a hug. Her mother's younger sister had always been Sam's favorite. With her soft voice she often appeared to defer to Nina Rae, but Sam had learned that was the secret to getting your own way much of the time.

"It's as if the whole idea for the shop were hers, isn't it?" Lily whispered in Sam's ear. Aloud she said, "It's beautiful, Sam. And everything looks amazing."

Lily's shape—so much like Sam's—attested to her love of pastries although Lily compensated well with her choices of expensive and flattering clothing. Sam wondered, more than once in her lifetime, how she'd managed to inherit more of her aunt's genetic makeup than her own mother's. Now if she could only remember to emulate Lily's fashion sense.

"Choose anything you want," Sam said. "Our signature coffee is very good, and I can vouch for the goodies too." She patted at her stomach.

"You've lost some weight, haven't you dear?" Bessie asked.

Since last night? "I sure hope so."

"Oh, that reminds me," Nina Rae said. "We all want to see your dress. I mean, *before* the official walk down the aisle."

No way was she walking into that minefield. Sam brightened her smile. "So! How about a couple of the butter cookies? Maybe a scone? Jen, make up a plate of treats and I'll get everyone something to drink. Coffee or tea, everybody?"

While they sampled several kinds of cookies Sam ducked into the kitchen and phoned Rupert. "Another zipper check," she whispered.

"Of course, sweetie. Ready now?"

I'm not sure I'll ever be ready. "Give me thirty minutes. Rupe, thanks. You're the best."

Back in the sales room Sam put her smile in place and stood by while the women showed off their purchases from the plaza shops.

"Too bad we couldn't talk Wilhelmina into coming along," Nina Rae said, dropping a lacy sweater back into her shopping bag.

Sam pictured her athletic cousin who preferred that everyone call her Willie. Hitting the gift shops with a group of women would be Willie's last desire in the world. In fact, they'd probably had a hard time convincing her to come to the wedding at all; Willie had never been interested in romance or marriage. Sam watched her mother, chatting with the other women at the bistro table.

Could that be the reason Nina Rae never used the shortened versions of either Sam's or Willie's names? Some things still weren't talked about very openly in her world. That could account for Nina Rae's being so relieved to meet Beau and pushing so hard for their wedding. It was bad enough to have such a masculine niece.

Sam shook off the feeling. Her mother came from a different generation, that was all. Deep down she knew that Nina Rae didn't harbor any bad feelings toward Willie or anyone else. She glanced at the clock above the counter. The zipper.

"Oh, gosh, I'm sorry to run out on you but I just remembered a delivery deadline. I need to get going," she said.

"Need any help?" Aunt Bessie asked.

"No, no, you all stay here and finish your afternoon tea. I'll see you tonight." She dashed out the back door, into her van and back to her old house.

Rupert was sitting in his Land Rover, reading through some typed pages.

"No problem," he assured her when she apologized for running late. "I'll have to do some revision on this new one before I send it to my editor. No matter how good you think you've got it, there's always some little thing to change."

He set the pages on the passenger seat and followed her inside.

"I didn't bring my body briefer with me, since I just dashed over from the bakery," she said, belatedly remembering the foundation garment. "But I need to know if this is even getting close. If not, I think we better call your friend the seamstress."

She stepped into the dress and called him into the bedroom. The zipper slid up. Not easily, but almost to the top.

"I think another three pounds and I might actually breathe at the same time," she said cautiously.

The box. She'd handled it yesterday. Could it be?

Chapter 7

The heavenly scent of grilled meat wafted across the back deck and into the house, and Sam smiled at the sounds of their guests laughing and chatting outside in the mellow September evening. Kelly chopped tomatoes and added them to the big salad bowl on the kitchen counter.

"I'm happy for you, Mom. Really glad you met Beau."

In comparison to Jake? Sam decided not to read too much into her daughter's comment. It only mattered that *she* knew she'd made the right choice. Jake the charmer with his changeable moods, or Beau the solid, honest man who loved her above all else. There was no comparison.

"Thanks, Kel. I can't believe how lucky I've been this past year." A picture of the wooden box popped into her head. Had it played a big role in bringing her that luck?

Kelly nodded as she added a chopped avocado to the salad. "True. A lot of great things have happened for you. Including having me move back home."

Sam rolled her eyes. "Including that. But don't get too cocky."

Chants of "steak-steak-steak" rose from the back deck.

"We'd better be getting the rest of this food to the table, or there's likely to be an uprising," Kelly said.

"This is a Texas crowd. As long as the steak makes it to the plates we'll be okay."

She picked up tongs and pulled ears of sweet corn from the big kettle on the stove, stacking them on a large platter. Thick toast with garlic butter filled a couple of baskets, and a casserole with barbeque beans had just come out of the oven.

Bessie stepped into the kitchen. "I hope Chub can pry our bull-headed daughter away from your horses long enough to eat with us," she said with a laugh. "I'd really hoped she'd outgrow that stage by her teens, like most girls do. But *no*, she works with 'em all week and rides 'em for fun on the weekends."

"She's welcome to ride here, all she wants," Sam said. "Beau says these two don't get nearly enough exercise."

"Let's not tell Willie that until after supper." Bessie took the platter of corn Sam had set on the kitchen's center island.

Sam glanced out the wide windows that faced the pasture as she set the baked beans on the table. In the distance Willie stroked Old Boy on his velvety nose then turned toward the house. Sam had the feeling Beau had already given her cousin the go-ahead for all the horse-time she wanted.

Beau caught Sam's eye through the window and she pointed toward the laden table. He handed platters of steaks to Chub and Buster then reached for the rope on the large bell that hung near the back door.

The long dining table had been maxed out with extra leaves and it didn't take but a rabbit's hair, as her father would say, for everyone to get to their seats.

"Here's to Sammy and Beau," Howard said, raising his glass of bourbon. "Thanks for having us all out to your home."

Sam felt a warm glow. It meant a lot to her that her father liked Beau so well and approved of the home she would now call her own. But then, hadn't she known that he would? The fertile ranchland and barn, the horses and dogs, the big log house—if Howard Sweet could have ordered up an ideal spot for his eldest daughter, Sam knew this would be it. She pressed her lips together so they wouldn't tremble.

"To my lovely bride and her family," Beau said, with a warm hand on her shoulder. "I'm right proud to be here, as ya'll would say."

Somehow they all knew that he meant it with respect.

"Now let's eat this fabulous steak," said Uncle Buster.

Bowls and platters were passed and conversation waned.

"Day after tomorrow, Mrs. Cardwell," Beau said

quietly as he leaned toward her with the salad bowl.

She passed the bowl along and linked her little finger with his, under the table, for a quick moment.

"I love you, Beau. Thank you for being you."

"You two are gonna have years and years to moon over each other like that," Uncle Buster said in his usual good-natured challenging manner. "Now, don't let this dinner get cold."

Everyone laughed. Sam gave Beau's hand another squeeze.

As the plates began to empty and offers of seconds and thirds went unheeded, Sam nudged Kelly and the two cleared the way for dessert.

"I thought about making a special cake for tonight," she said as she carried in a stack of small plates. "But then I remembered that Daddy would probably disown me if there weren't pie with at least one meal. So, Sweet's Sweets is proud to present our own recipe for real, authentic Texas pecan pie."

She gave a small curtsy and Kelly walked in with two pies.

"Well, it's a good thing you said that," Uncle Buster said with a fake scowl. "Hanging's too good for a woman who don't serve pecan pie at a special occasion like this."

Sam let the remark slide. Buster's humor often missed the mark, part of the reason she and Rayleen had often called him Uncle Bluster when they were kids.

While Kelly cut and served the pie, Beau leaned toward Sam again. "We gonna tell them tonight?"

"Oh. Yes, definitely." She tapped on her wine glass

with her fork. "We have a little change of plans to announce."

Nina Rae's face froze.

"No, Mother, you will be relieved to know that we are not cancelling or changing the wedding date. Sorry, I should have rephrased my introduction."

Her mother's expression lightened.

"We have changed our travel plans for the honeymoon. We're going to Ireland."

Voices erupted from every side of the big table.

"The trip is courtesy of Uncle Terrance."

At least half the faces wore puzzled expressions.

"Mother, you confirmed for me the other day that there was a great-uncle of mine in Galway, Ireland, and although I don't remember him myself, apparently he remembered me. And I'm surprised to say, he remembered me in his will. The trip is from him."

A dozen more questions came at her, but Sam had to admit that she didn't know much more than she'd already told them.

"I can't say anything more, other than 'let's eat pie'." She gave a shrug and took up a forkful of pecans in their sticky filling.

Beau offered after-dinner drinks and Buster and Willie went out to the back deck for a cigarette with theirs, while Lily insisted on helping Sam and Kelly in the kitchen.

"I'd keep news of this inheritance down if I were you," Lily said as she rinsed another plate and handed it to Sam to put in the dishwasher. "Your little sis is going to have a cow over the fact that she didn't get something too."

"I don't *know* that she didn't get anything," Sam said, fudging the truth just a little.

Hardgate had said the inheritance went to one niece in each branch of the family, which actually would cut out Rayleen. But until Sam knew more, including whether the bequest was even worth arguing over, she didn't intend to allow it to become a battle. She would split the proceeds with her sister if it amounted to anything.

Nina Rae's mouth seemed a little pinched when Sam emerged from the kitchen, massaging lotion into her hands.

"Coffee, Mother? I've got decaf."

"No thank you. Your father and I need to be going. I wouldn't want Zoë to think it rude of us to come in late at night."

Were the battle lines already being drawn?

"Zoë's used to all sorts of guests. I'm sure she doesn't keep tabs on when everyone comes and goes."

"Be that as it may, we'll be leaving shortly. I just need to say goodbye to Bessie and Chub."

"Mother—"

But Nina Rae already had her purse strap over her arm and was halfway to the door. She gave Bessie a quick peck on the cheek, snagged Howard's elbow and they were gone. Sam sighed. But she wasn't going to stress over it. The week had enough built-in stressors without spending time worrying over her mother's never-ending tendency to read drama into every little thing. She'd long ago given up trying to please everyone.

However, despite telling herself to stop analyzing, to simply focus on getting through the next few days with her sanity intact, she found herself thinking of ways to temper the situation. No doubt there would be talk in the family about Sam being the sole heir to whatever it turned out to be. She probably shouldn't have told them about it.

She dozed fitfully until her alarm went off. Rolling toward Beau's side of the bed she discovered that he was already up. She still wasn't used to the fact that he sometimes got emergency calls during the night and awakening to an empty house was going to happen now and then. However, a strip of light at the base of the bathroom door confirmed that he hadn't left yet. The light clicked off and she heard the door quietly open.

"I'm awake," she said. "Let me turn on a lamp for you."

"Sorry. I didn't mean to disturb you."

She pulled herself out of bed, explaining why he was the least disturbing person in her life at the moment.

He wore his rancher clothes—jeans, plaid shirt, roper boots. "Thought I'd tend the horses early and try to finish my day at the office in time to help out with whatever you need me to do today."

"Have you seen my checklist? I feel like there are a million things and a dozen people I have to satisfy before I can relax."

"Don't let your mother get you down," he said, wrapping his arms around her. "They're only here a few days and then we're off on our trip. And I'm going to make sure that your family members are the least of your worries during our honeymoon."

She gave in to the luxury of leaning into his warmth for a full two minutes. How was it that he read her so well?

Beau went downstairs, where he greeted the dogs in his gentle voice, and she heard the back door open and close. She picked up her jewelry box from her end of the long dresser and held it close for a minute. As always, the surface warmed to a golden glow and the small cabochon stones of red, green and blue began to sparkle. *Energy— give me the energy to get everything done today.*

The wedding checklist was on the kitchen counter and she scanned it while the coffee brewed, scratching through a couple of things she'd already done, leaving Beau a note about helping Zoë and Darryl with the rented tables and chairs.

At Sweet's Sweets Julio's Harley and Becky's minivan were already there when Sam drove up. Bless them. The smell of cinnamon and sugar greeted her, and she was pleased to see trays of scones and muffins already on the cooling racks.

"What are you doing here?" Becky asked when she spotted Sam.

"I'm not staying long. Figured I would put the finishing touches on my cake, since you've got your hands full with regular orders. After that, I have a few things to do." She held up the list, which now ran two pages long with only a third of the items crossed off.

Jen walked in as Becky was shaking her head over the enormity of it.

"And this is a simple wedding, right?" she said.

"Way simpler than most," Sam agreed.

"My mom did a lot of the planning for me," Becky said. "I was so young and all I knew was that I wanted a fantasy wedding. At least Mom had a clue how much they could afford to spend on it which, with two other girls coming along after me, wasn't much."

Sam rolled her eyes at the thought of the extravaganza Nina Rae would have put together.

"Well, I better get the front door open," Jen said, picking up a tray of cinnamon rolls moments after Julio had finished spreading them with glaze.

Sam put her list on her desk and went to the fridge where she picked up the fondant-covered tiers and carried them to the worktable. Adjusting her mindset—from harried to creative—she began piping complex scrollwork. In the background she was aware of the front door opening and closing, Jen greeting customers, her quiet voice as she made suggestions and rang up sales. Sam settled into a peaceful place, savoring the work and the smoothly running business she had created.

She finished the piped garland and the rows of precise gold dots that added finesse to the edges where the tiers met, and had just begun to trim rolled fondant into lengths for the ribbons that would drape from top to bottom—casually elegant.

"Sam?" Jen stood just inside the curtained doorway. "That man is back. Jake. What shall I tell him?"

How about, *go away. This isn't a good time.* But there wasn't really going to be a good time, when it came to Jake Calendar. And Sam couldn't leave it up to Jen to get rid of him. She would need to do that herself.

She sighed. "I'll be out shortly. Give him a muffin or something."

The last of the muffin disappeared into Jake's mouth when Sam walked into the sales room two minutes later.

"Jake. You're back."

"Yeah. How's everything going?" He shifted his weight to the other foot. "I enjoyed spending time with Kelly the other night."

A customer came in and Sam nodded toward the door, indicating that she'd rather take the conversation outside. They stood on the sidewalk under the purple awning that shielded Sam's display windows from the morning sun.

"Kelly came home somewhat upset," Sam said.

"I like that about you, Sammy. You're so protective."

"Damn right." She fixed him with a firm mama-bear stare.

"Look, there really wasn't anything to get upset about. I tried calling her afterward. I don't know what set her off."

"Really? Making a scene on the street in her hometown wasn't worth getting her blood pressure up, just a little?"

"That was dumb. I shouldn't have yelled at the guy. It's just, you know. In this business you get hit on by wannabe no-counts all the time. I didn't want him interrupting my time with my little girl. I was hoping to have a great evening with Kelly and that she would have so much fun she would suggest that you and I make up, maybe see more of each other . . ."

Seriously? Hadn't they already been over this ground?

She thought of Vic Valentino—a little 'out there' and somewhat humorous in his intensity, but everyone deserved a little respect. Jake didn't have to humiliate the man.

"Jake. It's not happening. We meant a little something to each other once. A very long time ago. I haven't even thought about you in years."

"You don't even have *some* fond memories of me?" The blue-green eyes sparkled, reminding her for a tiny moment what she'd found appealing about him.

She shook her head. "My life is full and happy now. I'm getting *married* tomorrow."

"I'd like to come, to bring you a gift."

"*No*, Jake. Go on back to California and have a great life."

"Sammy, Sammy, have a heart. We mean something to each other. We had a baby."

Don't play that card, Jake, don't even go there.

"I'd like to have you and Kelly in my life."

She felt her temper start to rise. "No! Jake. *We* did not have a baby. *We* had a hot little fling more than thirty years ago. *I* had a baby. *I* gave birth, *I* was up all those nights when she cried, and I practically slept through my series of crappy jobs during the day while I struggled to earn enough to feed her and send her to school and afford braces."

"You never *told* me about her. I would have helped."

"With *what?* You drifted. You told me the stories, back then, how you loved working a job until you had enough money to leave, how you never stayed one place long enough to grow roots or let some woman tie you down. It was a matter of pride, Jake, and you weren't going to change your ways because of me or a baby."

"But, Sam, a baby changes everything."

"That's a song title, Jake. And yes, it changes *almost* everything. But not *you*. You would have never stuck with us."

"She's my daughter, Sam." The blue-green eyes turned pleading and Sam felt her temper rise.

"One sperm does not a father make. Aside from your eyes and your hair, she's got nothing in common with you," she said through clenched teeth. "She's a grown woman now. Older and more mature than the 'I'm just reliving my youth' chickie you had on your arm the other day." She started to turn away.

"Don't you feel like you owe me a little something for all the years I missed out on?"

Owe me? That's what this was really all about.

"Owe you *what?*"

"A little birdie says you've come into some more money, Sammy. Nice little lady last night talking in the hotel bar with her husband, going on about how wasn't it romantic that *the kids* were getting this trip to Ireland for their honeymoon? Wasn't it fantastic that Samantha got that inheritance? It didn't take a rocket scientist to figure out it was you she was talking about."

Her expression froze.

"Sammy, I want you to meet our producer, Tustin Deor. Come on, you got the money from selling that art book."

How did he know about that? He must have researched quite a lot before he uncovered that fact. The thought chilled her.

"Sammy, that thing had to go for at least a million. And now there's more. You gotta be rolling, baby." He reached for her hand but she pulled back.

He thought she'd gotten a million dollars for Pierre Cantone's book of sketches? It wasn't even close to that.

"Tustin will be in town this weekend, just for a day, scouting talent, getting things finalized to go live with the show."

"I'm leaving on my honeymoon. And I don't care about your show."

"Sammy—"

She caught a dangerous glint in his eye.

"Don't you *dare* do anything to mess that up for me. Get out, Jake. Don't you show up at my wedding—I don't even want to see you hanging around Taos, and I sure don't want to hear your sleazy ideas or how bad you've got it financially. Get a job, a real job, and do what everyone else does. Save your money."

She felt a little twinge of guilt. She hadn't exactly earned the money to start her bake shop. The famous artist's sketchbook had come as a nice reward for solving a murder. But she'd been on the job when it happened, and she'd put her life in danger to find answers. And the inheritance . . . she still had no idea what that might consist of. The two windfalls had merely come at convenient times in her life.

Jake stared at her. He'd picked up her thoughts just

now, spotted that vulnerable little place inside her. His opportunistic little mind went to work, she could tell. He would never leave her alone as long as he thought she had some money.

"Maybe I'll touch base again, after you're back from your trip," he said with a devious little smile.

"Don't even think about it. Leave me alone, or else." She turned on her heel and yanked the door open. How on earth was she ever going to get rid of him?

Chapter 8

Her heart rate had accelerated to that of a hummingbird and Sam felt her face flush as she stomped back into the bakery. She crossed the sales room without meeting Jen's eye and flung back the curtain to the kitchen. Picking up the pastry bag she'd set aside earlier, she found that her hands were shaking too badly to work. *Piece of crap Jake. He shows up wanting to make me feel guilty because I won't give him money? I'm not buying into that.* She blew out a puff of air and picked up one of the fondant ribbons to place it on the cake. Her eyes welled up and she couldn't see what she was doing. A tear plopped onto the yellow fondant.

"Sam, what is it?" Becky asked softly.

Sam dabbed her sleeve at her eyes. When she focused again she saw that Jen had stepped into the kitchen.

"Don't let him upset you, Sam," she said gently.

Julio held a spatula, like an armed warrior ready to do battle for her.

"Look, everyone, it'll be fine. *I* will be fine. Probably just a case of bridal jitters."

"Sam, this isn't about the wedding," Jen said. "That guy has been here to see you twice now, and he's left you upset both times. Who is he?"

Sam laid down the fondant ribbon and took a deep breath. "He's Kelly's father."

She swore a collective gasp went up, but it was more likely just her imagination.

"Jake Calendar is his name. I knew him a whole lot of years ago when I worked at the pipeline camp in Alaska. We were young, a flirtation led further, and well . . . When I found out I was pregnant I left the job and came here. He knew nothing about Kelly until this week, and it's had everybody a little upset. I suppose I should have told the two of them earlier but I didn't and that's just the way it is."

"Does Kelly . . .?"

"I don't think she wants him around, but that's for her to decide. He wants money for a business scheme and I just want him to quit asking me for it."

"I could call some guys I know," Julio said. "You know, scare him a little."

"No! I don't want any trouble over this. Really, everyone. It's nice of you to worry about me, but he'll go away. Once the wedding is over and I'm away on my honeymoon, this will all seem very silly. I'm just stressing too much over everything."

"It's easy to do right before you get married," Becky said.

She launched into a tale of how upset she got because her party favors had come in the wrong color and there was no time to send them back, and it took Sam's mind off her own little drama. She drank a glass of water and went back to her cake.

Thirty minutes later she announced, "All we have to do is put the sugar flowers in place right before we take it to Zoë's in the morning."

"It's definitely the best cake you've done," Becky said, pausing in her own work to circle the near-finished piece and admire it. "I love the beading, the piping, the elegant draping. The flowers will top it off perfectly."

Jen came in to pick up a tray of brownies Julio had just finished. "Oh my god, Sam, this is gorgeous. I love the fall colors. Everyone is going to go crazy for it—it's perfect!"

Sam glanced up at the clock. "Oh gosh. Speaking of *everyone* I'm supposed to be having lunch with the ladies. I've got to get out of here or I'll never hear the end of it. Can you guys put the cake into the fridge for me?"

In the bathroom she switched her baker's jacket for a clean blouse and grabbed up her pack and keys. Missing this luncheon was not an option, as her mother had talked for days before they arrived about how much fun it would be for all the *girls* to get together. Plus, Sam had some fences to mend. Kelly had to work because her boss, Riki, had jury duty, and Rayleen wasn't in town yet so it would be Sam, the aunts and her mother. She drove toward the plaza where Aunt Bessie was to be waiting in front of the hotel.

"Good morning, dear," Bessie greeted when Sam pulled up to the curb in her colorful bakery van. Bessie's blond hair was perfectly styled, as usual, and her blue eyes showed no hint of Nina Rae's little snit from the night before. "You look very rosy today."

Was the altercation with Jake still showing on her face? Sam glanced at herself in the rearview mirror. Deciding her aunt was merely being nice, she shoved the rest of her concerns aside.

"I worked on my cake this morning. It's nearly finished," she said as she navigated her way around the plaza square and out into traffic.

"Oh—I can't wait to see it. Sam, you're going to be a beautiful bride."

It was one of those things everyone said to every bride. But it was nice to hear it. She reached over and squeezed Bessie's hand.

The restaurant was only a few blocks away, a place chosen by Nina Rae. Sam had never eaten there but knew of it by reputation and because she'd delivered cakes to the back door on a few occasions. Nina Rae, Lily and her cousin Willie stood in the tiny lobby, along with a surprise.

"I asked Zoë to come, dear," Nina Rae said. Her mouth still held a bit of the miffed expression she'd worn last night.

Sam sent Zoë a quizzical glance and got a small shrug of shoulders in reply.

"Mother, could we—?" Sam tilted her head toward

the exit. Without waiting for a response she placed a hand on her mother's shoulder and steered her to the door.

"Be right back," she said quietly to Zoë.

Outside, she led Nina Rae to a shaded spot a few feet from the door. A light breeze ruffled her hair.

"Okay, say it." She faced her mother. "Is it this business about that inheritance?"

Nina Rae's shoulders stiffened.

"Because I don't know that I'm getting anything at all, other than a plane ticket. If it turns out to be something valuable you know I'll share it with Rayleen. Probably with Willie too. But what if it turns out to be a property that has a lot of expenses? Does everybody want a share of those?"

She didn't wait for an answer.

"Mother, this week is supposed to be happy for me. Can we let unanswered questions rest, at least until we know what's involved? Please?"

"Why, Samantha Jane, of course I want this week to be a happy one. I don't know why you would think otherwise." At least the tight lines around her mouth had relaxed.

"Good." Sam glanced toward the door. "Let's go join the others."

Back in the restaurant's lobby she sent a subtle thumbs up to Zoë and Zoë returned a small wink just before they were shown to their table. White linens at lunchtime, full place settings, two crystal glasses at each place. Sam began to think she should have dressed up a little more, but then glanced at her cousin. Willie, the girl who was more comfortable on a horse than in a restaurant, any restaurant, was staring in dismay at the array of table finery.

"Willie, you'll have to come out to our place and visit the horses again," Sam said, taking a seat beside her cousin. "I think they miss you."

Willie smiled and visibly relaxed.

"So, Samantha Jane, when am I going to see your beautiful wedding dress?" Nina Rae asked from the other end of the table.

Sam pictured the zipper, not yet fully closing, and reminded herself to go by and try it on again. It was getting to now-or-never time. If the thing didn't fit today, she would have to rush it over to Rupert's friend and beg for a mercy alteration.

"Nina Rae, you know it's bad luck to see the bride in her dress before the wedding," Lily said.

"Oh, sis, don't be silly. That's for the groom. Certainly not for me."

"The cake is nearly ready," Sam said, putting a bright little note into her attempt to change the subject. "I think you'll love it, Mother. All the autumn colors you like so well."

That sent the discussion off to the subject of what everyone else was wearing, which got them through ordering their meals and the delivery of beverages to the table.

"Now, Samantha, I want you to let me know how I can help. I feel like I haven't done a thing to get you ready for this, and I can't believe you handled all of it without a wedding planner."

"I think it's all under control, Mother." Sam's teeth ground together. She was in middle school again, with her mother's reminders about her homework every single night. She forced herself to relax.

"The bouquets?"

Sam saw her chance for a peace offering. "Oh gosh. Maybe you could pick them up in the morning? I'll give you the directions."

That netted a smile.

"And your photographer? Will he be there on time?"

"We're keeping that informal. Rupert is an excellent photographer and he'll take most of the photos. But anyone who wants to snap away can certainly join in. The more the merrier when it comes to pictures, right?" Sam turned to Zoë for a lifeline.

"Darryl is putting disposable cameras on all the tables."

"Oh, I like that," Lily said. "Informal shots are always more fun."

"Oh! Speaking of which—" Nina Rae reached into her purse. "We need pictures of the luncheon. Since Rayleen couldn't be here."

Sam wasn't sure how showing her sister pictures of an event she couldn't attend was going to make her feel better about it. Just as Sam felt sure Rayleen would hear about the inheritance before anyone found out if it actually existed. She tamped down the thought and smiled when instructed. Luckily, their meals arrived just then and Sam turned the conversation to ask what everyone planned on doing for the afternoon.

"Well, we visited most of the galleries yesterday," said Lily. "And aside from one little place where Bessie found something she wanted to go back for . . . I'm not sure."

Sam told them about several interesting museums, including Kit Carson's house and the home of the former governor where a dramatic escape had taken place during the Pueblo Revolt. That should keep them busy for an afternoon, but if they tired of history they could always visit the D.H. Lawrence House or the Mable Dodge Luhan place for a dose of culture. Willie seemed torn between revisiting the horses at the ranch or checking out the Carson house where the famous frontiersman once lived. At least Sam had dodged the idea that they might all come over and watch her try on her gown. She left half the food on her plate and skipped dessert and decided she was as ready as she would ever be.

Outside the restaurant, she left Bessie with the others and, pointing them in the direction of the nearest museum, escaped. She still needed to get back to the bakery to put the flowers on her cake, slip by Kelly's to try on the dress, and make a few calls about some of the details which she would never admit to her mother that she'd forgotten. It was already well after one o'clock and she had to be back at Zoë's at five for a quick rehearsal, after which the family planned yet another restaurant meal—a welcome for Rayleen's family and unofficial rehearsal dinner.

As the van idled at a traffic light Sam debated how to allocate the time. Would it be worth a quick dash out to the house to call for help from the wooden box? She decided it would and turned on to Paseo del Pueblo Norte, hitting the speed dial number for Kelly on her phone. A quick reminder about tonight's dinner.

At the house she ignored the Lab and border collie as they dropped their toys at her feet and hoped for a game of fetch.

"Sorry. In a minute." She let herself inside and dashed up to the bedroom.

The wood sent warmth through her arms and into her body as she held onto the box and closed her eyes to absorb it more fully. After a few moments she set it back down. This exercise was more to test whether the dress was going to fit than to give her hours of boundless energy. People would notice that.

Back outside she tossed a ball for each dog, then got into her van and left. The morning replayed itself in her mind as she headed toward the center of town. Jake and his never-ending pleas for money. *Why me, and why now?*

It occurred to her that there was something more going on in his life. He'd hinted at financial problems— gambling, maybe? Drugs? Woman problems with the terminally cute Evie? Surely Tustin Deor and his ilk could come up with the money for their new project without coming to average people like Sam—wasn't that what venture capitalists did? If these guys were so well connected, they certainly had a lot of other ways to finance their show. She resolved to put the whole thing out of her mind. With any luck Jake would give up the quest and leave town.

The little house was dim and quiet when she arrived, empty feeling without her personal possessions even though she'd left the furniture and nearly all the kitchen gear for Kelly. In her former bedroom she debated whether to call Rupert for assistance with the dress again. Bless him, he was agreeable as ever and said he could be there in ten minutes. She tossed her clothes on the bed and pulled on the body briefer she'd brought along. Stepped into the gown and adjusted the cap sleeves. When Rupert pulled the zipper, it slid effortlessly up. All the way. Without a hitch.

"Girl, I think you've got it." He asked her to turn around. "Oh my. This is absolutely fabulous. Take a look."

He turned her toward the full length mirror on the closet door. All at once Sam remembered why she'd chosen this dress. The champagne-colored fabric and the tiny pearls gave her skin a radiant glow, and the skirt just grazed the floor when she stepped into her shoes.

Thank you, she whispered. Was it the influence of the box? She didn't care. The gown fit and she was happy for any little advantage to make it so. She twirled in front of the mirror and gave over to the relief and joy that flooded her. It was a major item, now off her checklist.

As soon as Rupert left, she carefully hung up the dress and made sure the veil and shoes were nearby. Kelly would meet her here tomorrow to dress for the wedding. Her wedding. It was finally going to happen.

She gave a deep sigh and suddenly felt tired. Relief from the whole week's stress flowed through her and she sat on the edge of the bed. Her eyelids became heavy. Just for a minute, she told herself as she stretched out and let them close. Just one little minute . . .

A persistent sound came through a dream about trying to find their gate at the airport. In the dream it was some kind of pager but when Sam's eyes snapped open she realized it was her cell phone. She sat upright, her heart pounding. What was she doing here? Patting the bedspread she located the phone.

"Darlin' are you on the way?" Beau asked. "Everybody's here."

Here? Oh my god, she thought. Zoë's place. The rehearsal.

"I'm nearly there," she said.

She leaped off the bed and grabbed up her pack, her heart pounding. In the mirror her face looked sleep-puffy and her hair stood up in disarray.

"How did I go so totally out of it?" she said to the room.

She ran her fingers through her hair and raced for the back door. Luckily, Zoë's house was only a couple of minutes away. She steered into their long driveway and jerked to a stop. Beau, Zoë, Darryl, her parents and the minister were standing beside the vine-covered pergola where the ceremony would take place.

"Sorry," she said, breathing hard. "I was—"

"It's okay, darlin'."

Nina Rae gave her a don't-be-irresponsible look. Her father merely looked as if he'd rather be watching a ball game on TV.

The minister, a man Sam didn't know aside from the fact that he'd officiated at Beau's mother's funeral earlier in the year, looked a little impatient. She sent him an apologetic look and took her spot where he indicated.

She blinked her eyes and willed herself to focus.

The whole run-through took about fifteen minutes and everyone seemed glad to be done as the sun set and the evening air began to chill.

"Everything okay, darlin'?" Beau asked as they walked toward Zoë's cozy kitchen where she'd announced there was hot cider.

"I just crashed," Sam told him. "I guess after all the pent-up stress, my body finally said you're going to rest. Already I feel better. And . . . the dress fits!"

He wrapped an arm around her shoulders. "Good. And I'm glad you're relaxing." They held back as the others went inside. "Do you realize that by this time tomorrow we'll be on our way to catch our flight, Mrs. Cardwell?"

She turned toward him and let the kiss linger.

"My mother's probably staring out the window," she murmured against his lips.

"Want to give her a show?"

"No!" She leaned back and looked into his ocean blue eyes. "Sneaking off would be more tempting, but we better stay sociable."

They linked hands and went inside.

"Now what time are we meeting for dinner?" Nina Rae asked as soon as Sam stepped into the warm kitchen.

"Soon. Have we heard from Rayleen's group yet?"

"They got in about an hour ago and your daddy said we would pick them up at their hotel, right Howard?"

He nodded, poking a slice of cheese into his mouth.

Beau touched Sam's elbow. "I need to stop by the office and make sure everyone's got their assignments for the weekend," he said. "Shall I come back by here to pick you up?"

"I'll just meet you up at Chez Monique. That way you don't have to hurry." Her parents had insisted on paying for dinner at the fanciest place in town, and this one with the somewhat pretentious French name fit the bill. Located on the side of the mountain overlooking town it was noted more for the prices and décor than for the quality of the food. "I can ride up there with Zoë and Darryl and we'll come back for my van later. Mother and Daddy are picking up Rayleen and Joe Bob and the boys."

Sam helped Zoë neaten the kitchen after the others trekked out. "So far so good," she said. "Mother isn't driving you crazy is she?"

"Other people's mothers usually don't. I think we're only affected by the buttons our own mothers know how to push. Don't worry."

Darryl was pulling on his jacket. In his teddy-bear way he was always a calming influence and Sam knew by watching them that her father had liked the big contractor right away. "You ladies almost ready?"

Her parents' Towncar was already in the crowded hillside lot and Darryl pulled their Subaru in beside it. The vestibule of the alpine-styled building was empty and a maître 'd led the way through the main dining room to a side room that had been set up specifically for their party.

"Oh my *lord*, Sammy!" Rayleen's voice rang out above all others. *"Look* at our bride!"

She had no clue how much she sounded like their

mother, Sam decided. In the five years since they'd last seen each other it was amazing how much Rayleen had begun to look like her too. No doubt that was the very same shade of Clairol.

Rayleen rushed forward with a big show of hugs and kisses.

"So, where is that handsome man of yours?"

"He'll be along any minute. A few last details at the office."

"This place—it's gorgeous! I bet ya'll eat here all the time. I know I would."

Joe Bob, the football jock from high school who had rapidly gone round in the middle, stepped forward and pulled Sam into a smothering hug.

"You look good, Sammy. A few extra pounds really fills out a woman like you," he said.

She backed out of the embrace and stared at his gut. Ignore it, she thought. Just remember how well that dress fit this afternoon.

He caught her stare. "Yeah, well. I sure don't get out to the gym like I should," he said. "Hey, how 'bout those Cowboys this season? Great start for them, huh?"

"Joe Bob, don't bring up football," Rayleen said. "You know it's a big old sore spot with the boys right now." She gave a glance toward the two teens who sprawled in chairs at the table with glum expressions and earbuds. She looked apologetically at the group. "They're not happy about missing Friday night football at home, that's all."

Buster and Lily showed up just then, along with Willie and Lester, so the little circle of cousins was complete.

Exclamations for Lub and Chub reminded Sam exactly why she'd never once considered moving back to her hometown. If you weren't enchanted by football or cotton crops, or thrilled by semi-annual trips to Dallas to shop for clothes at Neiman-Marcus, you absolutely didn't fit in with her mother's crowd. Sam put on a bright smile and gave a little wave toward her nephews.

"Everyone, let's take our seats," Nina Rae announced. She began directing. "Let's have our bride and groom right there, in the middle of that long section, so everyone can visit with them."

Sam resisted expressing a preference and sat where she was told.

"Where is Beau anyway, Samantha?"

"He'll be along." She glanced at the doorway. His quick stop did seem to be taking longer than expected.

Kelly appeared and her eyes widened a tad. Sam motioned her inside.

"I know, the crowd's a little intimidating," she whispered in Kelly's ear as her daughter took the seat on her right.

"Have I ever seen them all in one place at one time?"

"It's been years, probably."

"Even when I spent time at Gramma's in the summer, I don't remember all these."

Sam went into the short version of which ones now lived in Oklahoma, and which in what parts of Texas. "And of course Willie moved to Colorado, gosh, about the time I came to Taos."

Chairs scraped and when a waiter appeared with small

plates of bread and tiny bowls of oil for dipping, a rush of muscular arms reached out from all sides. Sam leaned back in her chair, intent upon ignoring the calories so her dress would zip again tomorrow. A young man dressed in black began taking orders for drinks and Sam sensed that the air in the room had changed. She glanced up to see Beau at the doorway. Something was wrong.

He made eye contact and tilted his head toward the exit. As Sam stood he mouthed, "Kelly too."

She touched Kelly's arm to get her attention away from Rayleen who was going on about how cute Kelly's hair would be in a different style.

She met Rayleen's gaze. "We'll just be half a second. Kel?"

Beyond the door Beau waited. "Let's step outside for a minute," he said, his eyes sweeping the half-full dining room.

"You have me a little worried," Sam told him as the brisk air hit her.

He took a deep breath. "At the office just now, there were a bunch of calls over the scanner. I put in a call to Taos PD to see what was up, whether I needed to send my men. It's a fatality over at the La Fonda. I hate to say it so bluntly but, it's Jake Calendar."

Sam felt her mind cloud over. Glancing at Kelly, she saw similar shock.

"He's dead?" Kelly said in a tiny voice.

Chapter 9

Sam had to clear her throat before words would come out. "What happened, Beau? He was healthy as a horse. Wasn't he?"

"The investigation falls to the municipal authorities, not my department. We're county. So I don't know many details. At this point they're only saying that they're treating it as a suspicious death."

"Well, I would think so," Sam said. She glanced toward Kelly whose face was very pale in the evening light. "When will you know?"

"That's just it, darlin'. I have no authority to go in there. And you know how Pete Sanchez feels about me. Sometimes his guys are cooperative, sometimes I get the feeling they are under orders not to be."

A year ago, when Beau's previous boss lost his job for covering up a crime after having an illicit affair, Beau had won the sheriff's position by default. The sheriff's cousin, Pete, the current police chief, somehow deemed it Beau's fault and now seemed determined to throw roadblocks up every time their paths crossed.

"About all I can do is have some of my guys keep their ears open, see what we can learn that way."

Sam turned to Kelly. "Honey, I'm sorry. Even though he—"

Kelly blinked hard, twice. "I barely knew him but still . . . It's hard to imagine this." Her voice was small and shaky.

"I know. I know." A chill passed through Sam. "Is there something we should be doing, Beau?"

Beau shook his head. "I can't think of anything, really."

Sam's head swam. Jake had mentioned some wives. Didn't say anything about children. It could be that Kelly was his next of kin. She'd tuned Jake out the minute he began asking for money and had never given him much chance to talk about anything else.

Memories crashed over her like waves in a storm— Jake's infectious smile and flirtatious eyes, their warm nights together, the decision to leave him behind and make her own life with her baby. Regrets: never telling him about Kelly, being short tempered with him in the past few days, perhaps not taking his request for the money seriously enough. They'd gone different directions, made separate lives for themselves. She knew a life with Jake would not have been a peaceful one; his displays of temper in recent days proved that. But still, she felt the loss of him, knowing he was now gone from this world.

Kelly walked ahead, Beau took Sam's hand—back into the restaurant, beside the tables of strangers. In their private dining room she could tell that Joe Bob was on his second beer and her father was nearing the bottom of his bourbon glass.

"Sorry for the delay," she said, mustering as strong a smile as she could.

Her mother sent her a funny look and Sam knew she was in for a round of questions later.

Beau deftly changed the subject and soon had the men telling hunting stories. She pressed Kelly's hand under the table and both of them tried to act as if everything were normal. Eventually the long dinner was over and she used the excuse that she had a lot of details to tend to so that she and Beau could go home alone. He made another call to his office but didn't learn anything new about Jake's death, and she found that between the upsetting news and the fact that she'd napped all afternoon she couldn't sleep until well after midnight.

* * *

Saturday morning. Her wedding day. Sam woke with Beau's arm around her, snug and content within the walls of their home. She looked at her left hand, half hoping that the wedding had already happened, wishing they could leave their normal world behind and start the honeymoon right now. But her third finger wore only the garnet ring he'd given her for their engagement and she knew their gold bands were still in her jewelry box, waiting for the afternoon ceremony.

Beau moaned and nuzzled close to her neck. She smiled. Life would be this, every day from now on.

"I gotta get the chores done early," he murmured, kissing her ear and rolling over.

And life would be *this*, she reminded herself. She had her own set of chores to do, although today the little jobs would be joyful ones. Sweet's Sweets, to finish her cake; Zoë's place, to deliver and set it up; Kelly's house to gather her clothing; and back to Zoë's to help with any last details and put on her dress. Beau had his own checklist, first to review the ranch duties with the neighbor's son who would look after the place while they were gone, then to pick up his Western-cut tuxedo and be at Zoë's on time. She sat on the edge of the bed and surveyed the little stack of items, including her underwear and jewelry, that she needed to take with her. She gathered the things and put them into a tote bag.

At the bakery, the crew were already well into the normal Saturday bustle. Sam pulled her cake from the fridge and gave it a close inspection. As upset as she'd been yesterday while placing the fondant ribbons, only the one teardrop had actually hit the cake. She pulled a tiger lily from the rack of sugar flowers they'd made and covered the spot. A quick image of Jake flashed through her mind. What had happened to him yesterday?

No. I am not going there. Today is for me and Beau. Whatever was going on in Jake's life, it was certainly not part of hers.

She finished placing the sugar flowers, a sumptuous bouquet of lilies, mums and daisies on top of the cake and clusters of smaller mums and daisies at each tier. With the yellow fondant and russet and burnt orange accents, it fit the autumn wedding theme perfectly.

"It's fabulous, Sam," Becky said with a smile.

"I love it. I'm glad it turned out so well. Now, did Jen put the notice on the door about closing early? You guys plan on being out of here by one o'clock. The ceremony is at two. And you know where Zoë's B&B is, right?"

Nods from both Becky and Julio.

"Do you need help with anything, Sam?" Jen had stepped into the kitchen.

"Kelly is bringing makeup and hair stuff. I have no idea what she plans to do to me, but I told her she better keep it tasteful. Wearing makeup is not my usual thing."

"Yeah, but you'll be happier with your pictures if you've added at least a little color," Jen said. "Just saying. Lipstick can be a girl's best friend at times."

Sam picked up her cake. "Okay then, I'm out of here. You guys have it for the next two weeks. Don't let the place burn down." She stopped short. "Not to put a hex on it or anything."

Becky laughed. "We'll be fine. Let me get the door for you."

With the cake safely stowed in the back of her van and the oversized tote bag containing her jewelry box and other items on the passenger seat, she took a deep breath and headed for the B&B. When she pulled down the long drive to the back the sight took her breath away.

Beautiful at all times, the acre surrounding the large

adobe bed and breakfast had been groomed to perfection for the wedding. Darryl had raked leaves from the spacious lawn where rows of chairs now waited the arrival of the guests. The log pergola was decorated with strands of silk flowers woven among the natural foliage. Sam saw Zoë's hand in the large pots of purple, orange and yellow chrysanthemums on the flagstone patio. Long tables with crisp white cloths stood ready for the buffet food and round dining tables were set up for the meal.

"Hey there, bride and cake lady," Zoë greeted as she stepped out the back door. "What do you think?"

"You guys . . . I don't know what to say. It's fabulous."

"Your mother approved it too," Zoë said.

"Is she—?"

"You just missed her. She said something about making sure Rayleen's boys brought suitable clothes."

"Knowing my sister, they did. Where shall we put the cake?"

Zoë opened the door and showed Sam an open spot on the kitchen counter, out of the way of the other food preparation.

"And here is a place you can call your own, for getting dressed, hair and makeup and all that," she said, showing Sam to an empty guest room.

"I thought you were full up right now."

"Some folks from Kansas were here for two nights but left early this morning. I had the room cleaned right away."

From down the hall came the sound of a football game on TV. Her father had apparently avoided having to go out with the ladies by retreating into a favorite pastime.

She peeked into the den and said hello.

"Do you have time for a cup of tea?" Zoë said as they walked back to the kitchen. "The kettle is already hot."

Sam checked the time. "A quick one. I told Kelly I would meet her here at noon. For some reason she wants a couple hours to make me presentable. I still have to run by the house and get my dress and see if I've left anything else behind."

Sam tamped down the zillion questions that had been racing through her head: had they ordered enough food from the caterer; would Kelly remember her checklist; would her mother try to change the floral order; would the dress fit as well today as yesterday? She closed her eyes and let the tea soothe her.

"Well, I better get moving," Sam said when her cup was empty.

Out in the van she dialed Beau's cell but didn't get an answer. His list of errands was nearly as long as hers and he may have left the phone lying around somewhere. At her old house she let herself in and tossed her pack on the kitchen table.

I have to know, she thought. She went to the bedroom and slipped her clothes off quickly then stepped into the gown. As it had yesterday, the zipper moved effortlessly closed. Her eyes rolled heavenward. *Thank you.*

The front doorbell rang, startling her. No one ever came to the front door. She hiked up the wide skirt and tiptoed through the house. *I'm not speaking to anyone who's selling anything.*

A police car sat out front. Town of Taos, not one

from Beau's department.

She opened the door a few inches.

"Samantha Sweet?" Two men stood on her porch, one in uniform, the other in a suit. The suited one had asked the question.

"Yes?" She looked at their faces. Both were vaguely familiar as occasional customers in her shop.

Suit Guy held up a badge wallet. Detective Raul Ordonez.

"We're looking into the death of Jake Calendar," Ordonez said. "May we ask you a few questions?"

He stepped forward, assuming Sam would let them in. She backed into the living room.

"You don't seem surprised to learn that Mr. Calendar is dead," he stated, eyes scanning the layout of the house.

The uniformed officer glanced into the kitchen and the short hallway leading to the two bedrooms and bath. Sam watched the officer closely, not really wanting to give him access to the house.

"I heard. Last night. Sheriff Cardwell is my fiancé."

"Not for much longer," Ordonez said, tilting his chin toward her gown.

"The wedding is in two hours, actually, and I'm supposed to be on my way. So, what can I do for you?"

"We have a number of questions."

"For example?"

"Where were you yesterday afternoon between two and five o'clock?"

"I was right here."

"Anyone with you? Someone who can verify that?"

"No—I stopped by to try on my gown. A friend came by to help me with the dress."

"For three hours?"

"After he left, I got sleepy and laid down for a nap."

"He?" His insinuation was clear.

"It's not like that—he's not interested in women." Sam explained who Rupert was and the man seemed momentarily satisfied with her answer. It wouldn't matter. She knew, as she was talking, that Rupert could only swear to being with her for a few minutes of the whole afternoon.

"And no one else came by or called you during that time?" Ordonez was writing notes in a small spiral notebook; the other officer had moved back to the front door.

"Where are you going with this? I don't see how it relates to your case."

"You had an argument with Mr. Calendar yesterday morning. There were witnesses."

Sam's gut clenched. Could someone have construed their discussion as a threat? It was ridiculous and she told him so. She rubbed her bare arms against the chill in the shaded house.

"Would you be more comfortable in your regular clothes?" Ordonez asked with a sympathetic expression. "We can wait a minute while you change."

She did feel a little ridiculous being questioned in her wedding gown. "Yes, thank you."

In the bedroom she quickly put the dress on its hanger and got back into her jeans and the striped cotton shirt she'd put on this morning. She glanced over at the telephone on the nightstand. She should call Beau and tell him about this. Rapidly punching in his cell number, her heart beating faster, she waited. It went to voice mail again and she left a quick message.

A tap at the door. "Ms. Sweet? Please come out."

She set the receiver down and opened the bedroom door. The uniform guy stood there and she held her ground until he retreated again into the living room.

"After your argument with Mr. Calendar yesterday, what happened?" Ordonez smiled, keeping his tone friendly, although Sam knew the questions were deadly serious.

"It wasn't really an argument. He wanted to borrow money, I said no. After he left I finished some work at my shop and went to lunch with relatives who are in town for the wedding. After that I came here and tried on the dress and fell asleep."

"And that's all?"

"When I woke up I realized I was running late for the wedding rehearsal so I dashed over to that. From that point on I was with a lot of people throughout the evening."

His pencil scratched away at the notepad.

"All of them, including Sheriff Cardwell, can verify that," she insisted.

"I'm sure they can. It's just that . . . that one stretch of time that you can't account for."

"I did account for it. I was right here."

"It gets a little more complicated than that, Samantha.

May I call you Samantha?"

She gave an impatient nod.

"We should really discuss this at the station. We'd like for you to come with us."

"I'm getting *married* in an hour and forty-five minutes! Can't this wait until another day?"

"Not really." He held out a hand, ushering her toward the door.

"Wait a second. I'll need my bag and keys," she said, ducking around him and heading to the kitchen for her pack.

She locked the front door behind them, eager to figure out what they really wanted so she could get back to her plans.

She rode in the back seat of the cruiser, feeling a little unsavory. How could she keep the day on track with this nonsense going on? She pulled her phone from her backpack and called Kelly, telling her to go by the house, get the dress and take it to Zoë's. When she said she'd been delayed, Kelly jumped to the conclusion that she'd gotten tied up at the bakery and Sam let it go. There was no way she wanted to get into explanations. Surely this couldn't take more than a few minutes.

The cruiser drove past the plaza and turned on Civic Plaza Drive. Sam's face burned with the knowledge that someone she knew might see her in the police car. Her hands weren't cuffed but as they walked her through the back entrance of the police station, Sam couldn't have felt more like a perp. Her blood pressure kicked up as the place closed in on her.

"Your pack, ma'am," said an officer just inside the

door. "Scanner. It's procedure."

She set her pack on the conveyor where it didn't set off any alarms, but when Ordonez unzipped the top and spotted her passport he paused.

"Going somewhere?"

"Yes, on my *honeymoon*! It's an old tradition, right after a couple are married . . ."

He gave her a look that told her she better shut up. The envelope from Clinton Hardgate came out next and he held it up, his eyebrows arched.

"Beau and I are going to Ireland. Tomorrow."

Ordonez handed her pack to her but held on to the passport and tickets. "We'll see."

Sam felt like screaming. Surely he couldn't do this.

"You'll get them back. I only have a few other questions." He led the way to a room with a small glass window inset in the door and ushered her inside. "Have a seat."

She remained standing and crossed her arms. "My wedding starts in less than an hour and a half. I've answered your questions. I need to go."

Ordonez met her gaze steadily. "Not yet."

He pulled open a large paper bag and from it withdrew a plastic evidence bag. "Our crime scene people were at the La Fonda nearly all night, processing the scene. Do you recognize this?"

Inside the evidence bag she glimpsed a very familiar shade of purple—a small bag from Sweet's Sweets, with her logo on it, a little crumpled.

She took a shaky breath. "These sacks come from my bakery. Every customer who buys a small item usually gets one."

"Do they usually get one with your fingerprints on it?"

"What are you getting at? Where did you get this?"

"From Jake Calendar's hotel room."

"So? He did come into my shop. He bought a few things." Although, as she recalled, Jake usually wolfed down his pastries before he got out of the shop.

The detective set the bag down. "This particular item seemed to be made especially for the victim. Once we have autopsy results we can verify our suspicions."

"*What* suspicions?"

"The indications are that Mr. Calendar was poisoned. By a cupcake from your shop."

Sam felt her mouth fall open.

"You also seem to have left out one significant detail when you failed to mention that Mr. Calendar was the father of your daughter."

She closed her mouth and sat down.

Chapter 10

Sam caught a glimpse of Chief Sanchez through the small window in the door leading to the corridor. The chiseled planes of his face seemed set in smug satisfaction. A frisson of fear went down her spine.

"I want to make a phone call," Sam said.

"You're not under arrest. Relax. We're just talking."

"My wedding . . . The guests will be there by now." Beau would be in his tux, Zoë setting up the cake, everyone waiting on her. She could imagine the look on her mother's face. Kelly trying to reassure her grandmother while wondering what on earth had happened.

"I can send a squad car over to let them know about the delay," Ordonez offered, for all the world sounding like he wanted to be helpful.

"No! Do *not* upset my parents with this. Let's just get the questions over with." She worked to keep the panic out of her voice, picturing Pete Sanchez behind the two-way mirror, gloating over messing up Beau's wedding day.

"Here's what it looks like to us," Ordonez said, fixing her with a hard stare. "You and Jake Calendar had an intimate relationship. He came to town. You say it was to ask for money, but maybe there was a hint that he would expose that relationship to your fiancé or your family."

Heaven forbid that her mother learn about Jake Calendar through the police. Sam realized she should have gotten all of it out in the open years ago.

He read her expression too well. "That concerned you. You wanted him out of the way, figured a little something added to a pastry . . . He would believe the pastry was a kind of peace offering or something so he wouldn't hesitate to eat it . . ."

Sam knew she should call a lawyer. But whom? The only attorney she'd spoken to in years was Clinton Hardgate in New York. And he only dealt in wills and trusts. Locally, she'd revised her own will a few years back. That firm would be of no help either. She had no clue who to call on a criminal matter.

Her phone rang down inside her backpack. She reached for it before Ordonez could stop her.

"It's my daughter. I'm sure everyone is frantic. Let me just tell her I'm delayed."

"*Only* that."

"Kelly, the police have a lot of questions about Jake's death," said Sam in a rush. "Tell everyone we have to postpone the ceremony until four o'clock."

She barely got that out before Ordonez grabbed her phone away. He shut it off and laid it on his side of the table.

"What? I didn't say anything I shouldn't have."

A tap came at the door and Ordonez nodded to someone through the window. Again, Sam spotted Chief Pete Sanchez. Ordonez picked up all the items on the table, including her cell phone, and left the room. She eyed the mirror on the opposite wall, certain that she was being observed. After all, she had stood behind the two-way mirror in Beau's department a time or two when he had interrogated someone. She did her best to appear calm. It was probably a losing effort. Minutes ticked by.

When Ordonez returned he went right back to his notes.

"Now, you say you went directly from lunch at The Willows to your house to try on your dress. How, then, is it that your vehicle showed up on a traffic camera on the north end of town?"

"There are traffic cams in Taos now?"

He gave her a hard stare. "Temporary ones. Ms. Sweet, is that really all you took from that statement?"

She pressed her knuckles to her temples, thinking. The past few days had been so busy— "I went to Beau's— to the home I now share with my fiancé, who would be my *husband* by now if you hadn't come along—to get something. Then I came back and tried on the dress."

"We've been unable to reach Rupert Penrick to verify that."

"Because he's at my wedding. Waiting for me!"

"I can send someone over there to speak with him, if you'll tell me where it is," he said in a perfectly reasonable sounding voice.

No! The word resounded through her head. This whole thing was going in circles.

"What else?" she asked.

"Can you explain how the bag from your shop—with your fingerprints on it—got to Jake Calendar's hotel room, with a poisoned cupcake inside it?"

"Any paper bag from my shop could have my prints on it. I often unpack shipments of new ones and resupply the stack under the sales counter. At this point it seems you are jumping way ahead. You won't even know for sure how he died until you get the autopsy results."

A flash of irritation crossed his face. The detective clearly didn't like her questioning his assumptions. He stood again and left the room.

Another detective came in, a woman who identified herself as Mira Schwartz. If Ordonez was the good cop, Schwartz was playing bad cop. She ran through the same set of questions, then threw in a new accusation.

"If you know nothing about poison in a cupcake, how is it that you very conveniently have a can of Ratzout in your vehicle?" Schwartz's mouth settled into a hard, straight line.

"I use it in my business," Sam said, realizing two seconds later what a mistake that statement had been.

"Obviously," said Schwartz with a grim little smirk. "Poison and baked goods seem to go well together, for your purposes."

Schwartz left the interrogation room and Sam thought about simply getting up to find out if that door was locked, but she wasn't sure how far she would get. Plus, they still had her things.

Time dragged by. Clearly, they were trying to wear her down by making her wait. She'd tried every calming technique she could think of to keep herself from screaming.

Eventually, Ordonez came back in and Sam heard raised voices out in the hallway. She knew one of them.

"Beau! I'm in here!" she shouted, dashing to the door and pounding on it.

He appeared to brush off whomever he'd been speaking with as he opened the door.

"Sam, come on. We're leaving." He stared at Ordonez. "You had no right to hold her here all this time. Tell Sanchez this is not over."

"He's got my phone and my passport and our airline tickets," she told Beau.

Beau stood straight, regal in his tuxedo, and stared the shorter man down. Ordonez led the way into the hall and down to a desk. He picked up a large plastic bag, reached into it and retrieved Sam's cell phone.

"The passport and tickets have to stay with us," he said. "She's a suspect and, with these, a flight risk."

Beau's jaw muscle twitched but he didn't say anything. He took Sam's elbow and steered her toward the exit where his Explorer waited in the parking lot. It was dark outside and Sam shivered in the chilly air. She hugged herself against the cold and felt her eyes well up.

"I've missed my wedding," she said bleakly. A sob escaped.

"Darlin' it's okay. We'll straighten it out." He opened the passenger door and guided her into the seat, closed her in securely and got behind the wheel.

"How did you know where—?"

"Kelly got your call about being delayed and then I thought to check my messages." He started the engine. "I'm so sorry that my phone was off when you called. When you said the police were at the house I started calling around. At first nobody would tell me where you were, but I finally reached somebody helpful. One of my former deputies who switched over to the PD. He scouted around and told me you were at the station being interrogated."

"I thought they would just ask a few questions and it would be quick. I kept thinking I could get back to the wedding. What happened there?"

He gave a rueful glance. "Well, the minister had to leave. He had another wedding this evening. By mid-afternoon everyone was getting hungry so Zoë and the caterer put out the buffet and that kept them happy for awhile. I managed to make them hold off on the cake. It's safely locked inside Zoë's office."

"Everyone went home?"

"Yeah. The relatives are all settled back at their hotels. Poor Zoë was getting the third degree from your mother, but I tried to let them all know that everything would turn out just fine."

"I can't face them right now," she said.

"You don't have to. We're going home." He'd already

turned away from the center of town and headed north toward the ranch.

Sam's thoughts churned, reviewing everything that should have happened by this point in the evening. So many things to reschedule. Among the first on the list would be to contact Clinton Hardgate and be sure the travel reservations were changed so they weren't permanently lost. *Damn the local cops*, she thought. *You aren't messing up both my wedding and my honeymoon.*

She was astonished to see, when they walked into the house, that it was after nine p.m. She phoned Zoë and reassured her that she was all right. Zoë offered to pass that along to the parents so Sam wouldn't have to get into a long explanation. The next call went to Hardgate's cell number and she was half surprised when he actually answered.

"I know it's late on the coast," she said.

He was gracious about it and told her not to worry about the travel plans. He would place everything on hold and wait to hear from her again. Although she hadn't given the reason for the delay, he wished her luck.

"What would you like? Are you hungry? Or maybe just some wine or tea?" Beau asked from the kitchen.

"A shower first. Then maybe a cup of hot chocolate." Sam couldn't think of anything at the moment beyond getting rid of the scummy feeling of the police station.

When she came back downstairs fifteen minutes later, fluffing her hair to dry it, wearing soft pajamas, Beau handed her a mug of cocoa and she snuggled into her favorite corner of the sofa.

"We can set the wedding up for tomorrow," he said. "Same time, same station."

"I can't do it, Beau. I can't stand the idea of starting marriage as a murder suspect."

He went completely still. "Did they actually say that? What all did they ask you, darlin'? Go through the whole thing."

She did, covering every question, every answer, and everything Ordonez had said to her. As she talked he paced the room.

"Damn. I wish this were in my jurisdiction. Even though I couldn't work the case myself—because of us—I'd have ways to find out what's going on behind the scenes, to know what evidence is coming out."

"Until they get the autopsy results, they won't know for sure that Jake was poisoned or that the poison came from the cupcake, will they?"

He looked thoughtful. "Well, they probably have a pretty good idea about the poison. There are signs on a body. They may even know what type it was. But the medical investigator's office in Albuquerque will verify it."

"They can't really think that I, or any of my crew at the shop, really did it though. That would be so stupid. My business would be ruined if—oh, god, what am I thinking? If word of this gets out, my business will probably be ruined anyway. People won't buy pastries at a bakery if somebody died from our product, will they?" Despair crept in.

"Don't get ahead of yourself, darlin'. We can only take things a step at a time. I'll call the O.M.I.'s office myself tomorrow and see if I can get answers. If their findings eliminate you as a suspect, I'll go down to the PD and demand your documents back."

Sam had a horrible feeling it wouldn't be quite that simple.

Chapter 11

Another sleepless night. Sam stared at the ceiling until nearly dawn. She felt Beau's eyes on her. He moved in close and held her, but it didn't help a lot. She'd ruined their wedding plans.

No, she told herself. Jake Calendar ruined their wedding plans. He'd made someone mad enough to take revenge. It was just ill-fated timing that it happened in her town and right after they'd had words. The thought of Pete Sanchez's bad feelings toward Beau and the way Ordonez and Schwartz had looked at her as they asked their questions—the whole thing made her feel sick inside.

At dawn they gave up the pretense of sleep.

"Come outside with me," Beau said. "Let's breathe

some fresh air and get your mind off everything else."

He got up and started pulling on his clothes. She followed on semi-automatic, not really because she thought it would help but because it was a relief to simply follow, not to have to think or plan.

A light frost lay on the pasture grasses and the dogs trotted along beside them as she trailed Beau along his well-worn footpath to the barn. He dipped a bucket into the feed bin and handed it to her.

"Here, Old Boy likes this oat mix. Hold it out for him." He scooped another bucket for the mare, Pretty Girl, and they walked out to the wire fence where the two horses stood in the chilly air.

As the animals nuzzled into the buckets Sam focused on the little things—the way the mare's hair formed a whorl around the white patch on her forehead, the way steam rose from their nostrils when they raised their heads and chewed.

"How about a short ride?" Beau asked.

Without waiting for an answer he headed into the barn and came back with a saddle and tack. Within minutes he had Pretty Girl saddled for Sam and a blanket thrown over Old Boy's back. He helped Sam with her stirrups, then saddled and mounted the other. They set a leisurely pace, riding the fence line around the fifteen acres.

Frost crunched under the horses' hooves. Steam rose from the grass wherever sunlight struck, melting ice crystals into dew. In the trees two vivid blue jays got into a ragged conversation, and a raven cawed as it soared overhead. Sam felt her head begin to clear. It was easy to forget your worries out in the blue-gray dawn air. She let out a contented sigh. If only life could stay this simple, always.

The phone was ringing when they walked back into the house. She felt her mood deflate. Beau picked it up.

"Zoë," he said, handing the receiver to Sam.

"Hey, girl. You okay?" She didn't really wait for an answer. "Just FYI, I wanted to let you know that your mother and sister have started the day on a mission. They're determined to see the wedding go through—today."

"Oh boy." Sam could see the female dynamos of the family orchestrating to fix what they felt were Sam's failings in the planning department.

"Do you want to come by and talk to them about this?"

No. Not at all. "I guess we better. Can you get them through breakfast and we'll come down there in awhile."

Zoë chuckled. "Breakfast is what we do here. Don't worry about it. I'm sure Darryl and I can think of ways to stall them even longer if you want us to."

"I have to deal with this sooner or later," Sam said. She could hear the resignation in her own voice.

Beau figured out what Zoë had said.

"Let me call Albuquerque and see if I can get someone I know on the line at the O.M.I.'s office. Somebody will be at work there, even on a Sunday."

Sam put coffee on to brew while he dialed. In a minute or so he signaled her over and put the phone on speaker.

". . . chocolate cake, ingested between three and four p.m. with death occurring within minutes afterward. The poison was cyanide, commonly found in rat poisons or several other household products used to kill vermin," the male voice said.

"Any other trauma to the body?" Beau asked.

"None. The poison was definitely the COD."

"Thanks, Dan. If you would, don't mention my call to anyone from the Taos Police Department. We're working a different angle of the case."

"No problem."

The line went silent.

"This isn't good," Sam said. "They already know that a chocolate cupcake came from my bakery. And they found Ratzout in my truck. Every year we get an infestation when the weather turns cold and I've doused my garage and several of my caretaking properties with the stuff."

"Half the stores in town sell Ratzout and a lot of homes have a supply of it," Beau said. "They'll never prove that you are the only one who could have poisoned Jake."

"But none of those other homeowners really had a reason to wish Jake would go away."

"One thing at a time," he said. "Who knows, maybe overnight they've found someone else with even a stronger motive. Let's just let it play out."

He poured coffee for each of them and made cinnamon toast with the last two slices of bread in the house.

"I better go face the music with my family," Sam said, brushing toast crumbs from her hands as she finished the small breakfast. "I can't leave it to Zoë much longer."

"I'll go with you."

"You don't have to do that. Besides, you can do more by trying to find answers and get my passport back."

He kissed her on top of the head and squeezed her shoulders. "It's going to be fine. I'll make some calls and be sure we can get the latest information. Maybe today they'll find the real killer. It'll be such a relief that you'll be ready to come walking down that garden path by this afternoon."

She wrapped her arms around him and fervently hoped he was right.

Ten minutes later, she knew he wasn't. Blue strobes flashed in her rearview mirror as she approached the plaza. She pulled onto narrow Bent Street and stopped at the curb. *Really? Right here in the middle of town?*

She powered down the window of her pickup.

"Samantha Sweet? I'm afraid you need to come with us, ma'am." It was Pete Sanchez, with an officer that looked like a rookie. The chief's face held a hint of humor. The bastard was enjoying this.

She felt like cursing, crying, screaming. But she got out of the truck, locked it, and walked with Sanchez to his cruiser.

* * *

This time she didn't say a word. They advised her of her rights, photographed and fingerprinted her. She kept her lips pressed together through the whole ordeal and was shown to a cell where a tired-looking woman in a see-through blouse and tight skirt that barely covered her buns sat on the thin mattress on a stainless steel bunk. An unflushed toilet sat in the corner. Sam felt her lungs tighten against drawing in the odor. The woman raised her head, took in Sam's freshly washed hair and clothing with hard eyes.

"What'd *you* do?" she asked.

"Nothing!"

"Yeah. Me too." She resumed staring at the floor.

An hour later a female officer showed up and ushered Sam down the corridor to a room where a man in a windbreaker waited at a table.

"Sam, hi. I'm Mark Nelson. Beau Cardwell called me."

She recognized his lean face from an ad on the cover of the phone book, one of those "If you're in trouble with the law . . ." ads she'd always found pretty sleazy. Now she was glad to see him. In jeans and a polo shirt, with the casual jacket, he looked like he'd been pulled away from a Sunday ball game with his kid.

"Beau says you're in some kind of trouble. Said he called me because he's watched me in court before."

That wasn't exactly a glowing recommendation, since Beau often complained about attorneys who twisted the facts to get guilty clients off. At least his voice was kind.

"Beau gave me the basics: you had a prior relationship with the dead guy and argued with him that day, he died from a pastry that came from your shop, your fingerprints were on the bag the pastry came in, and you don't have an alibi for the time of death. That doesn't sound good."

Her already-rotten mood plummeted.

"*But*, I don't think they have nearly enough evidence to take this to trial. Beau seems to think the Chief has targeted you to get back at him for some reason."

Sam started to open her mouth but Nelson held up a hand.

"It doesn't matter. What matters is that we can make a pretty good case for the judge to allow bail. You're a solid member of the community and shouldn't have to spend months in jail while they build their case."

Months? Sam felt her face go pale. How could her life have gone so completely haywire in less than a day's time?

* * *

"Bond is set at fifty-thousand dollars," the judge said on Monday morning, banging his gavel and calling for the next case.

An hour later Sam walked out into sunlight, with Beau's arm around her and his assurances that meeting the bond agency's requirements had not posed a problem.

"I'm so sorry I couldn't do better for you last night, darlin'," he said, helping her into his Explorer.

"Has any of this been in the news?" she asked, a twist of fear in her gut.

"No. The local reporters got wrapped up covering a suicide off the gorge bridge, and the Albuquerque stations have a lot bigger things happening in the city."

"What about my folks?"

He pulled out of the parking lot. "I've covered, saying that you were helping the police with some questions and that it was our mutual decision to put off the wedding for a few days. I kind of didn't tell them you were away from home all night. Your sister and her gang had to leave yesterday. Her boys have school today. The aunts and uncles are getting a little restless since they've seen all the touristy stuff already. I think some of them are getting ready to leave."

"Mother must be fit to be tied."

"Probably. Zoë says she's determined to stay until there's a wedding. Sounds like a shotgun situation to me." He winked and sent her a grin that lightened her heart.

"I better talk to Mother and Daddy," she said. "But first I have to get a shower and disinfect these clothes. I'm surprised you can stand to be in the car with me."

"I'd be anywhere with you." He reached across the console and took her hand.

He drove north, parked beside the house and walked inside with her. "Now, you take your time with a shower and do whatever you want. I'll go get your family and bring them out here. You can talk to them alone, or I'll be on hand for support if that's what you want."

She nodded. Watching him drive away she steeled herself against the shaky feeling that threatened to overtake her. She talked herself through the steps. Shower. Face the parents. Discuss wedding. Find Jake's killer. Of all those, she knew the last item was most important.

Forty-five minutes later, one step done. Sam felt better with clean hair and clothes although the knot in her stomach refused to go away. To keep busy she put together a light lunch for the others—salad and sandwiches—and was ready to set it out when she heard Beau's car coming up the drive. She drew in a big breath, watched Nina Rae and Howard get out, tried to read their expressions. Behind the Explorer was Chub's rental car. He, Bessie and Lily followed.

Her father appeared glum, his mouth downcast, his eyes very still. Mother was the opposite, eyes taking in everything, quick turns of her head, as if there might be photographers behind every bush waiting to capture their humiliation.

Stop it, Sam. Don't read too much into it.

Beau ushered them up the steps and opened the front door. Sam left the kitchen and met them in the living room.

"Mother, I—"

Nina Rae came forward and took Sam by the shoulders, giving her daughter the same perusal she'd done outdoors, trying to see if anything looked different. Howard stepped over and put his arms around both of them. The strange group hug broke off, leaving Chub and Bessie no alternative but to offer perfunctory hugs of their own. Sam had to wonder how much they knew about her situation. Finally, Lily. This embrace felt genuine, as her favorite aunt held her and whispered in her ear, "This too shall pass, honey."

Sam closed her eyes for a moment, working at composure.

Not to be outdone, Nina Rae moved in for a second awkward hug. It was a warmer welcome than Sam had expected, but then she remembered Beau hadn't exactly told them she'd spent the night in jail. Maybe they could continue to gloss over that little fact.

"I need to tell you some things," Sam said when they'd backed off a little. "Let's go sit down."

They complied—Sam imagined a little stiffly—taking seats on the sofa while Sam and Beau flanked them in the armchairs beside the fireplace.

"I don't know how much you've heard so I'll just start at the beginning. When I left Texas and went to Alaska that summer after graduation, I met this guy named Jake Calendar . . ." The rest of it came out easily enough, up to and including how he'd come to Taos recently and met his daughter for the first time. How some of his behavior disappointed Kelly and as far as Sam knew he'd planned to leave town and not pursue a relationship.

"Whatever might have been, it won't happen now. Jake died on Friday, I'm afraid under suspicious circumstances."

She glanced toward Beau and he gave her an encouraging smile.

"Then we come to this past Saturday," she said, taking a breath. "The police do have some evidence against me, but it's pretty circumstantial and my attorney believes they will end up dropping all the charges. Until they do, though, Beau and I feel that we should wait to get married." *Because what if they actually do manage to send me to prison?* She didn't say it.

"Charges? My lord . . ." Her mother's face had gone pale. "Samantha Jane, no one in our family has *ever* been arrested before. Well, there was that one time with Joe Bob in high school and them kids who got to drinking and carousing, but that was before he married into— See, what I *mean* to say is—"

Howard spoke up: "Let's just be supportive, Mama. Sammy needs us to love her and not judge."

Sheesh—*had* they been judging?

Chub looked to his brother. When he spoke it was to echo Howard's words. Bessie nodded too. Lily, who had been standing behind the sofa, slipped over to Sam's side and laid a gentle hand on her shoulder.

"Oh, Samantha, your daddy is right. I'm sorry," said Nina Rae. "We're behind you no matter what, honey. Daddy and I will stay right here in town as long as you need us."

Lily knelt beside Sam. "I'll send Buster on home. I can stay too."

"There's no need," Sam said, touched by the gesture. "There's really nothing anyone can do, except for Beau. He's got feelers out in law enforcement circles and we'll get the answers."

Lily held Sam's hand tightly. "Are you certain? Please, call us if there's *anything . . .*"

Bessie echoed the offer, then the three of them said their goodbyes. Sam watched, a lump in her throat, as the car pulled down the long drive.

"I meant what I said, no matter what anyone else does," said Nina Rae. "Your daddy and I are staying to get you through this."

To see that I really do get married.

"That's your call, Nina Rae," Beau said. "Sam and I will be pretty busy, though. It's obvious that the police aren't looking seriously at any other suspects, so it's going to be up to us to find out who really did this. I know your daughter." He sent a smile Sam's direction. "She's not going to give up and she's not going to sit by and hope for the best. She'll be working on this thing right alongside me."

No one brought up the fact that Chief Pete Sanchez could make that problematic for both of them.

Chapter 12

Sam didn't sit still while Beau drove her parents back to the bed and breakfast. She phoned Mark Nelson and requested a meeting, called the bakery to be sure things were running well and to reassure the employees that she was fine.

"Do not discuss Jake Calendar with anyone who comes in," she told Jen. "If the police ask questions, you'll have to answer. But do it privately and tell no one else. The business can't afford to get caught up in some kind of vicious gossip mill."

"Absolutely, Sam," Jen assured her. "I'll pass that along to the others."

Sam felt a little of her tension ease away.

"We can see the lawyer at three," she told Beau when

he came back. "What can we do in the meantime?"

They sat down with notepads and began to make a plan.

"First, who else in town knew Jake Calendar?" Beau asked.

Their list wasn't particularly reassuring: Sam, Kelly, and the girlfriend Evie.

"I'll track her down. Was she local or did she arrive with him from California?"

"California, I think."

"With any luck, maybe she has stayed in town. If the police didn't ask her to hang around, I will. I can make her believe I have the authority to do that." He stared at his page. "We still don't have much of a list."

"Wait, there's also that guy who tried to audition for him," Sam said. "Kelly said Jake publicly embarrassed him. That could be a motive. I can find him. He left a phone number when he ordered the cake."

"I wonder who's claiming the body," Beau mused. "Do you remember if he had family? Otherwise, it might be up to Kelly."

A responsibility her daughter didn't want or need. She tapped her pen against the yellow notepad.

"Way back, years ago, Jake talked about his parents some. But I got the impression they've been gone for awhile. I honestly don't remember anything about siblings. Jake mentioned being married more than once. I suppose we could try to find out who the ex-wives are." Would an ex really want this task?

Beau jotted a note on his list. "I can make an inquiry. My contact in the PD will surely let me know that much.

Hopefully, the victim's wallet or cell phone provided a contact."

"I wish I'd gotten specific information about this Tustin Deor he was working with. *If* that story was even true. Jake was always such a schemer. He might have been bullshitting that whole line."

They each had a page of notes and a couple of assignments. "We better get busy," Beau said. "Especially if I hope to get to Evie Madsen before she leaves town."

"I'll be at Mark Nelson's office at three o'clock. Join us if you can. I'm sure you can think of questions I should ask him."

"Mainly, what we want from him is to know what evidence the police have against you. If he hasn't started gathering it yet, be sure he shares whatever he gets, as he gets it."

She gave him a little salute and picked up her pack. The early afternoon traffic was light and she made it to the center of town within fifteen minutes. Parking her pickup truck behind Sweet's Sweets she spotted Kelly carrying a trash bag from Puppy Chic out to the dumpster. Kelly dropped the bag and ran over to hug Sam.

"Oh god, Mom, how awful for you last night."

"I'm okay. We're working on finding out what really happened. Meanwhile, we're not talking about this to anyone outside the family. Okay?"

"Absolutely. If you need any help. Anything at all . . ."

"I will let you know. Beau and I are hoping to find some answers today. Grandma and Grandpa are staying town until there's a wedding, and that can't happen too soon for me either."

Kelly nodded knowingly. "Just say the word."

Sam walked into her shop, happy to see that Becky and Julio were busy with their normal duties. Becky gave her a sympathetic smile.

"Zoë's husband brought your cake back. It's in the fridge."

"I'm sorry you guys wasted your Saturday afternoon," Sam said.

They gave the same reassurances she'd been hearing all day. Jen heard Sam's voice from the sales room and peeked through the curtain, adding her own good wishes.

"I need the order page for that cake we did last week, the audition piece," Sam said.

She went to her desk and rummaged through the folder of finished orders. Valentino's order was near the top and she jotted down the phone number he'd given. While she was trying to decide what approach to take when she talked to him, her phone rang.

"Sam? I'm so sorry to bother you with this now," Zoë said. "I just looked at my bookings. I'm full up all week, starting tonight, people who booked months ago."

"Explain it to my mother. She'll understand."

"Shall I send them to a hotel?"

Oh boy. After what she'd put them through already . . . Sam couldn't add insult to injury. "I'll have to clear space in Iris's old room, but that's doable. Have them pack up their stuff and I'll figure out something by this afternoon."

When, exactly, that would happen Sam had no idea. It was already after two and she had the meeting with Mark Nelson at three. And she needed to squeeze in a quick visit to Vic Valentino if she could find him. She dialed his number.

"Victor Garcia's residence," a young-sounding female voice said.

"I'm trying to reach Vic Valentino. Do I have the right number?"

"Oh my god, yes! You must be from *You're The Star*. He *really* needs this call. He was so upset the other night. He thought your judge rejected him, but now if you're calling back . . ."

This was one of those instances where giving the truthful response wasn't going to get her what she needed.

"I'd like to meet very quickly," she said. "Could I come by the house? I just need directions."

And just that fast, she had a way to find Valentino. She pulled up in front of the apartment the girl had described, a two-story tan stucco building full of sliding doors and narrow iron-railed balconies painted turquoise. The Del Ray Apartments might have once been a cheap motel, for all the building's charm. Unit 1-J was on the ground floor at the west end. A skinny sidewalk led to a courtyard of sorts, one that might have once been landscaped but now consisted of gravel and a few spiky agave plants that could gore you to death if you came home drunk one night. Sam tapped at the door.

Vic Valentino opened it and his smile drooped. "You're the bakery lady. Maria said you were from the show."

"Well, I didn't quite say that," Sam said. How much should she tell him? "I said I needed to talk to you *about* the show."

"Oh my god, I'm getting a second chance!"

Vic backed into the apartment and Sam followed, closing the door behind her. He paced the floor of the miniscule living room, taking three lengths of it in under a minute, mumbling something about what he would wear.

"Will this audition be for a different judge?" he asked, coming to halt in front of her. "One of those pretty girls I saw? I think I'd have better luck with female judges. Maybe one of them would see my performance now."

He must be talking about Evie and Kelly, who were both standing on the sidewalk with Jake when Vic received the grand rejection. Of course, he didn't know that Sam knew about that.

She shook her head. "Vic, I don't really have any inside information about the show itself. I was just wondering whether you ever got the chance to sing for Mr. Calendar."

"I tried to." He told her that he'd met up with Jake outside the hotel, glossing over the details that Kelly had told her, not mentioning the cake at all. "He was kind of busy at the time."

"Did you make another appointment to see him again after that?"

"I tried. I hung around the lobby of the La Fonda the next day. I thought about trying to take him another bakery present."

Her interest perked up. "Did you? Take him something?"

"Nah, I chickened out. He didn't exactly appreciate the cake like I thought he would. The guy turned out to be a total asshole."

Clearly he didn't like the way Jake had treated him— who wouldn't be resentful of that?— but Sam didn't detect the kind of anger that would drive Vic Valentino, or Garcia or whatever his name really was, to kill. This guy still had grand hopes for getting on the talent show. She would see if anything turned up on Beau's background check before completely writing him off. She talked her way out of Valentino's needy clutches and drove away from the Del Ray Apartments, deciding to cut through on Bent Street to reach Mark Nelson's law office without having to drive through Plaza traffic.

Shoppers filled the sidewalks along the narrow street and Sam slowed, knowing that in tourist mode it wasn't uncommon for some little old man to step out into traffic to get a picture of a crumbling adobe wall. A bright pink sweater caught her attention and she realized that the young woman filling it was none other than Evie Madsen.

Evie, it seemed, wasn't wasting a lot of time grieving for Jake. She was laughing at something a man next to her must have said. A horn tooted behind Sam's truck and she picked up her pace a little. So Evie was still in town.

Sam turned right at the next intersection, drove a block, and found the law office. Sitting in the parking lot she quickly dialed Beau's cell.

"I spotted Evie," she said, telling him where the girl had been walking.

"Good. When I called the hotel they couldn't tell me if she was still staying there. I'll cruise around and see if

I can pick her up and have a little chat."

Sam described Evie and her clothing, then gave him a heads-up on her parents' impending stay. "I better get to that meeting with Nelson now, but I'll go home after that and make the room ready for them," she told him.

From the street the offices of Nelson and Gravitz looked like any of a hundred other traditional adobe buildings in Taos. Mud brown walls, wood framed windows painted blue, wrought iron lettering spelling out the name of the firm. Inside, Sam discovered, the attorneys had given themselves the creature comforts that come with success. Deep leather sofas and chairs in the waiting room, heavy Mexican desks, custom crafted end tables, pricey art by Gorman and Peña. It was a man's world, one meant to let the client know why he was the loser and his attorney was the winner in life's lottery. Through their brilliance, this successful team would save you from prison and line their own pockets handily.

She hoped her own case would be resolved for less than the cost of a Gorman painting, realizing with a jolt that if the prosecutor really pressed it, she might have to sell her house to save her life.

She managed a wan smile at the sleek receptionist who greeted her. When the girl left to announce her, Sam blinked hard and gave herself a little pep talk. Financial ruin wasn't in her future. She and Beau would find out the truth.

She hoped.

"Samantha, good to see you again, under better circumstances this time. Did Chloe offer you some tea?"

"Thank you, no," Sam said. *No way I'm spending time on*

chit-chat with someone who costs nearly ten bucks a minute.

She followed Mark Nelson through a series of hallways which revealed a number of small offices and a lot more employees than she would have imagined. By the time they reached his private office and she'd taken a seat, she'd probably spent fifty dollars.

On the drive over, she'd thought of telling him exactly what she and Beau planned to do but decided against it. One, he might try to talk her out of doing anything and, two, she didn't want to pay to hear herself talk. She was here to get her hands on whatever information the Taos Police might have against her.

Nelson hesitated when she asked to see the file but he finally pulled it out. "If you were ever close to the victim, Sam, you won't want to see the photos. Death by poisoning isn't pretty."

"Beau will want copies," she said. "I'll settle for letting him look them over. Mainly, I'd like to know exactly what the police have that they feel warranted charging me with this crime."

"It's largely circumstantial," Nelson said as he flipped through some pages. "Cupcake from your shop, your prints on the bag, poison that you had readily at your disposal, and the big fight you had with the victim."

She didn't spend time refuting or explaining. That could happen if they ever had to prepare for a trial. Right now, she and Beau needed leads—any leads.

"The firm has a private investigator who handles the sort of thing you want to do," he explained. "He's a professional."

The tone said 'leave it alone' but she wasn't listening. Beau was better at investigating than ninety percent of the local PIs, and he had a vested interest in getting this solved quickly.

"Just the copies, please. That's all I need for now. We can plan strategy later, once we know everything we're dealing with." She offered up a wide smile with the request.

He stalled with more friendly-sounding advice, but she held her ground until he called an assistant in to begin copying the contents of the folder.

Chapter 13

"Darlin' I'm proud of you," Beau said with a grin when she handed over the attorney's folder. "I half expected him to pat you on the head and tell you to get your beauty sleep and just leave the heavy lifting to him."

"He did. But I karate-chopped his hand and then sat on him."

He laughed out loud; it was the first time in two days she'd heard that cherished sound. The two of them were in his mother's former bedroom, stowing boxes of her things that they hadn't sorted since she passed away in January, making closet space, dusting furniture. Sam had stripped the bed linens and found fresh ones in the closet. A candle and some flowers, and the room would be as nice for her parents' visit as any hotel. She couldn't match Zoë's fabulous breakfasts but she had a sneaking feeling her mother was about to commandeer her kitchen anyway. Biscuits and gravy for breakfast were her specialty; Sam thought of her waistline again and vowed to avoid them.

"I think I heard a vehicle," Beau said, walking to the bedroom door to peer out the front windows. He looked back at Sam. "Ready for this?"

She bundled up the old sheets and dashed to the laundry room beyond the kitchen.

"Woo-hoo, anyone home?" came Nina Rae's voice.

Sam took a breath, put on a smile and walked out to greet their first houseguests.

"Now I don't want ya'll to worry about supper tonight," Nina Rae said, holding up a supermarket bag. "We've got it all covered. Roasted chicken, sweet corn, and I bought the ingredients to make my famous coleslaw."

Sam's smile went plastic. The famous coleslaw was something of a family joke, as no one other than her mother actually liked it. She would have to warn Beau to take a small serving or be sure one of the dogs was sitting nearby.

Nina Rae bustled into the kitchen and began taking items from her shopping bag. Sam looked at the clock. Her dad would be ready for happy hour. Although Sam was itching to get on with the investigation she put the desire on hold long enough to get through drinks, dinner and an evening of chit-chat.

Beau's phone rang twice during the second of the *Seinfeld* reruns. Nina Rae cackled at the inside jokes while Howard dozed in one of the recliners. Beau excused himself each time and took the calls in the kitchen. When the second one came Sam sneaked in there too.

Beau thanked the caller and turned to Sam.

"Tustin Deor is in town, registered at the La Fonda."

"So, apparently this whole *You're The Star* thing is for real," Sam said. "I halfway believed that Jake was just blowing smoke, trying to get money from me for who knows what reason."

"I'll do some more background on Deor when I can get to my computer at the office. A basic search online just lists his publicist's version of his bio—movie credits and such—which I suspect may be just a little inflated. Once I have more facts about him, I'll stop by and question him a little, find out how things were between him and Jake."

"Tustin and Evie could leave town any day, couldn't they?"

"Apparently there's a press conference tomorrow afternoon. I don't know what he's announcing but it must be related to the show."

So, basically, Sam thought, we *might* have twenty-four hours in which to gather information about the people Jake was hanging around with, before they scatter and leave the state.

"Hey, you two," Nina Rae said. "I was wondering where ya'll got off to. How about we get up a little domino game? It'd keep your daddy awake until the ten o'clock news."

Sam couldn't remember the last time she'd watched the late news. With a schedule that included getting up at four-thirty, six mornings a week, bedtime in her home came pretty early. She'd forgotten how her parents' routine never varied. She stifled a yawn and gamely agreed to find the dominoes.

She flubbed most of her plays and fell way behind, but winning meant more to her mother, so Sam let it happen. Across the table, Beau kept making eye contact and she knew there was something he wanted to tell her. When the opening strains of the network news theme came on, they left the elder Sweets to it and said goodnight.

"I wanted to tell you about that other phone call I got tonight," Beau said as they were brushing their teeth at the double sinks in the master bath. "The police have found Jake Calendar's brother and he's coming to town to pick up Jake's belongings. Tomorrow."

"Will you get a chance to talk to him?"

"I hope so. It would be nice to know what else was going on in Jake's life. There are millions of people out there beyond Taos, and I can't help but think his death might not have anything to do with this little town at all."

Sam dried her face, hoping that was true. She didn't like to think that Jake's appearance here was the reason he died. On the other hand, why would someone from California track him here and then take such pains to make it look like Sam had killed him? Maybe she should start looking more closely at who her own enemies might be.

* * *

Sam's rocky night in that cell caught up with her quickly and she was asleep almost instantly after pulling the big comforter over herself. When she woke it was dark and the clock numerals read 3:41. Random questions came at her. Who might be angry enough with her to frame her for Jake's murder? Or was she simply being paranoid—maybe the cupcake was the handiest method for the killer, nothing at all personal against her? Like a broken record, the thoughts kept replaying in her head and by four-thirty she knew there would be no more sleep. She kissed Beau's bare arm lightly and rolled out of bed.

The bakery, as always, became her refuge. By the time Julio arrived she already had scones in the oven.

"Hey, boss," he said. "No time off?"

"I tried. Things are just too jumbled up right now."

He nodded knowingly. Normally a man of few words, he'd worked for her a couple of months already and still Sam knew relatively little about him. It was nice, after the long weekend with her family, to be around someone who rarely spoke. He set to work with the breakfast pastries while Sam organized her desk and checked email.

Not many messages; everyone believed her to be away on her honeymoon right now. She sighed at the reminder of how far off track their plans had gone. She should be in Ireland now, finding out about the inheritance from her mysterious uncle, she thought as she clicked on junk messages to delete them. She stopped in mid-click. What if—? No, it couldn't be—

She went back to the emails, but her mind kept jumping track. What if this sudden inheritance had something to do with Jake's death? Or, more specifically, with Sam being made to look like the guilty party. Who would know about it? Who would actually do something about it?

It was not quite seven, but on the east coast it would be two hours later and she felt sure Clinton Hardgate would be in his office. She dialed his number and walked to the empty sales room for privacy.

"Ready to reschedule that trip?" he asked after a quick greeting.

"Not quite." She had never told him the real reason for the delay. "I have a question, though."

She wasn't terribly surprised that he didn't know of anyone else in New Mexico who might know about her inheritance unless she had told them.

"Our firm would never divulge such private information," he said. "What's this about?"

"Probably just my over-active imagination," she said. "I ran into some trouble recently that got me thinking somebody might benefit if I were out of the way."

"Sam, do you think your life is in danger?" She got the feeling that he was picturing some Wild West scenario, where bad guys came riding into town and challenged her to a shootout.

"No, not really. But do let me know if you come across anyone outside my family who might have a connection."

For a fraction of second she toyed with the idea that it could actually be someone within her family, someone who believed they might get the inheritance if Sam were put away for life. But that didn't make a lot of sense either. For one thing, no one had known about it until the very day Jake died. And those who knew about the inheritance didn't know about Jake. And why harm a stranger when it was far easier to do away with Sam herself? And why do that when they could simply let her accept the money and then nag her to death for a portion of it? That scenario seemed far more likely.

She filed away that entire line of thinking and started toward the walk-in fridge. Her wedding cake was stashed it there, but Sam was beginning to think it ought to be in the freezer where it would keep longer. There didn't seem to be any quick solution to the mystery of Jake's death coming their way anytime soon. She had brought the cake to the worktable and found heavy plastic wrap to secure it when the front door bells jangled and she heard a male voice speaking to Jen. A few seconds later the intercom buzzed.

"Sam? Someone to see you."

She spotted a red BMW parked at the curb. At the sales counter stood a young man who looked vaguely familiar. Tight black jeans on a skinny frame, black silk shirt, short wool jacket—black, of course—and some kind of designer watch that looked like plastic but probably cost a few thousand dollars. His green eyes were narrow under heavy brows and his sable brown hair was gelled into an odd little point at the top. Another guy, dressed similarly but without the same air of *cool* had a cell phone to his ear, was speaking in the tones of some power-conversation. Outside, a burly man in black stood near the BMW.

"You're Samantha Sweet?" asked the first man.

She nodded and thought she caught a flicker of disappointment.

"Um, I'm Tustin Deor." He held out a hand.

He looked about eighteen, although Sam felt sure

he had to be in his thirties if Jake's version of his accomplishments were even half true. He regarded Sam down the length of his perfectly straight nose, reconciling what he saw with what Jake must have told him. Obviously he'd been expecting someone who oozed money without having to work for it—maybe some kind of society lady associated with the arts and willing to back their production if the star-power were strong enough.

Sam gave him as genuine a smile as she could muster. "Jake's friend."

"Colleague," Tustin said. "In a way. Jake wanted in on my latest project. I thought I'd see what he could bring to the table."

He leaned a hip against her sales counter, seemingly relaxed, but his gaze traveled around the room constantly.

He recapped the pitch, which was pretty much what Jake had told her several days ago. She let him talk.

"Last time I spoke with Jake," he said, "he thought you were pretty interested. Said you knew him from way back. I'm sure you knew that Jake was a pretty decent musician himself. We're gonna miss him. He said you loved music."

"Really?" She vaguely remembered him getting together with another guy at the pipeline camp, both of them strumming guitars and belting out Creedence Clearwater songs. If Jake ever did become a good musician it was well after those days when he couldn't stay on key for *Proud Mary*.

"Look, we're holding a press conference this afternoon on the plaza. Two o'clock, couple big announcements. Come by. I think you'll be impressed with what we've got going for us. You might change your mind about investing." He flashed a smile that probably worked wonders with rising young stars like Evie Madsen, then walked out and got into the Beemer. Not exactly broken up over the loss of his business colleague, *if* Jake had truly been important to the show at all.

"Whew—cute!" Jen said, giving herself tiny pats on the chest.

"Seriously?" *Man, I* am *getting old*, Sam thought as she went back to the kitchen to tend to her cake. She constructed a large box to hold the cake and then wound lengths of plastic wrap around it, musing over the situation.

None of this made sense. If this Deor guy was such hot stuff in Hollywood why were he and Jake scouting around Taos, especially around her, for money? Surely the kind of folks who backed half the other crappy reality stuff on television would follow Deor anywhere. Either Jake had painted Tustin a completely wrong picture of Sam's situation or Deor wasn't nearly the hotshot Jake had made him out to be. The old charmer at work again. Who else had he tried to swindle in recent times?

Across the table, Becky was working on a cake with a photography theme, which reminded Sam of the news conference Deor planned to hold this afternoon. She would remind Beau about it and suggest that they go and listen in.

She pulled her phone from her pocket but before she could dial him, it rang in her hand. Her mother's number showed on the readout. Sam knew what would happen;

bored with hanging around the ranch, the parents would cook up some activity for Sam to do with them. She understood that—they'd come to town to see her. But now that she had to clear her name or face a trial, it seemed there were more important ways to spend her time. If she and Beau ever hoped to be married and get on with life, they needed to devote their time to the effort of finding Jake's killer. Sam let Nina Rae's call go to voicemail and she dialed Rupert.

"Help, please," she whimpered.

"For you, love, anything. How's it going?"

She gave him a quick rundown of the situation since the wedding had fizzled. "I need someone to entertain my parents for the day."

"No problem. How would they like lunch and shopping in Santa Fe?"

"It sounds like exactly Mother's cup of tea. Just tone down the clothing if you can for my dad?"

"What—he's not into purple?"

Sam couldn't begin to explain how *not into purple* her father, the retired accountant, would be. "Maybe stick to the grays and blacks today, if possible, Rupe. Otherwise, whatever you can think of that would keep them busy all day . . . I would *so* appreciate it."

"Shall I pick them up at your place?"

"Let me verify that and I'll get right back to you."

She listened to her mother's message—exactly as she had guessed, they wanted to make lunch plans. When she called saying that a friend really wanted to show them around Santa Fe since she and Beau were tied up all day, Nina Rae readily accepted the invitation. Sam told them

Rupert would be there in a half hour, called him back and said anything in the world he wanted would be his in return for the favor. He jokingly said he would pass on her firstborn, thank you, but a heavenly dessert for one of his monthly soirees would be an excellent trade-off. She hoped he felt that way after a whole day with her mother.

Chapter 14

Her next call went to Beau, telling him about Tustin Deor's visit to the bakery and suggesting that they might want to catch the press conference this afternoon.

"Good idea. I've got more news. Jake's brother, Tom, will be in town this afternoon to get Jake's possessions."

"Can we talk to him?"

"I got a phone number. Thought if you made the call, explained—only as much as you want to—about knowing Jake from the past . . . maybe he would agree to see you. I can be there if you want."

"You could help me think of questions to ask him. It might be our only chance to find out what's been going on in Jake's life in recent years. Maybe Tom would know whether he had enemies out there somewhere."

She gathered her thoughts and called Tom Calendar. He was on the bus, just outside town, and explained that he planned to drive Jake's pickup truck home.

"I knew Jake a lot of years ago," she said.

"Yeah, I recognized your name. He talked about you a lot when he got back from Alaska."

"Really?" She felt oddly gratified for that scrap of information. "He'd stopped in at my shop last week. I'd really like to talk with you. Could I pick you up at the bus station?"

"That'd be great. Afraid I don't know the town at all."

He told her what time to arrive. Taos didn't really have a bus station, as such, just a lobby attached to a local business where people could wait for the next Greyhound. She ran a couple of quick errands and made sure she was there five minutes early. She called Beau and told him what she had planned.

Tom Calendar looked enough like Jake to make Sam's breath catch. Same hair, grayer—Jake might have been coloring his; the eyes had more green, less blue; his size and shape were nearly identical, dressed in jeans and a blue all-weather jacket. She got out of her truck as he stood beside the bus, looking around expectantly.

"Hi, Sam," he said, hefting the strap of a small duffle to his shoulder.

His voice was similar to Jake's, too, but without the quality that made you feel like you were being sold on something. She liked his genuine smile and waved him toward her truck.

"Are you staying overnight?" she asked.

"Yeah, a room at the Econolodge. Didn't have any

idea how long it would take me to . . . do what I have to."

She nodded. "Before you talk with the police, I need to tell you some things. Can I buy you lunch?"

He didn't have much choice since they were in her vehicle, but he didn't seem to mind. They pulled into the crowded lot at the Taoseño. An empty table wedged against the far wall looked like it would afford the privacy they wanted, although the room was so full of noisy diners there was little chance of their conversation being overheard. They asked for water and spent a few minutes looking over the menu.

"So, what was this you wanted to tell me?" he asked. Direct and to the point. She liked that.

"The police know that Jake and I were involved at one time, and they seem to think I might have killed him."

"I assume you didn't, being that you're sitting here with me. That you even *want* to sit here with me."

"That's right." She looked up and saw Beau walking toward them.

She gave Tom a two-sentence rundown on why she and Beau were investigating on their own. The two men shook hands and Beau took the empty seat next to Sam's.

"I wanted you to know," Sam said, "that no matter what might happen after this, including a trial if they take it that far, I didn't harm Jake. It had been a lot of years, and I didn't particularly have feelings for him when he showed up, but I would never wish him harm. He was my daughter's father."

A variety of reactions flickered across Tom's face but all he said was, "Okay."

"So." Sam let out a pent-up breath. "We need to find

out who really did kill him, and why."

Beau set his menu aside. "Oftentimes things follow a person around. We wondered if there was anything back in California, a person or situation, Jake might have been involved with, something that gave somebody a reason to come after him?"

Tom shook his head slowly. "I wouldn't know. Jake and me—we're brothers but we're not much alike. He always wanted adventure. Me, I'm a school teacher—eighth grade math. He loved the ladies, flirted a lot—three marriages. I've been married more than twenty years to the same woman, got two kids. Jake liked things flashy, went to Vegas a lot . . ." He spread his arms and looked down at the simple plaid shirt he wore under the windbreaker.

Three marriages? Jake had kind of glossed over that little fact. "Did you stay in touch?" Sam asked.

"Sort of. We only lived an hour's drive from each other. We'd call now and then. He'd send me a text, I'd email him pictures of the kids." He shrugged. "That's about it. No big, cozy Christmas dinners or any of that."

"He'd recently become involved in a television project, a reality show called *You're The Star*. Did he talk about that?"

"No, never heard of it."

"Back when I knew Jake before, he played guitar. Did he still have that interest in music? It might be what drew him to get involved in this type of talent search program."

"Yeah, he never gave up the guitar, although I doubt he ever learned more than a dozen chords. Volume over detail—that was more his style."

Their enchiladas arrived and they paused until the waitress had walked away.

"At one point, Jake formed a little band that he said would go big-time," Tom said. "He always had a group he played with—guys came and went all the time. But this once, they'd stayed together long enough to get pretty good. Did some bar gigs, even recorded an album. I always suspected that they paid for the studio time and bought all those tapes themselves. But Jake liked to make it out like they'd really impressed some music producer and that there'd be a contract coming along any day."

Tom ripped a tortilla in half and swabbed it in the red sauce on his plate.

"But that was Jake. He could sure tell a tale. Anything to put himself in the limelight. He wanted so much to be a star of something. That was kind of the sad part." His eyes grew distant. "He thought living in Hollywood would make him one of them."

* * *

By the time Sam dropped Tom Calendar off at the Econolodge it was almost time for the press conference Tustin Deor had told her about. She parked her truck behind Sweet's Sweets and walked the two blocks to the plaza.

A table was set up under the roof of the bandstand, with a row of chairs and a couple of microphones. A backdrop with repeats of a logo—a flying gold star with electric blue lettering proclaiming "You're The Star"—ran like wallpaper so that it would appear in any photograph that might conceivably be snapped. Outside the little fencing around the raised platform stood a gaggle of reporters with long lenses and big fuzzy microphones to keep the wind from messing up their sound-bites.

Parked along the sides of the plaza were at least a half-dozen vans, one for each of the network stations from Albuquerque and a few from cable news channels, the ones that spent their energy on covering the publicity-hungry world of personalities, those familiar faces that were famous for nothing more than the fact that they were famous. Sam was surprised at the level of media interest.

Near the edge of the group a couple of rough-looking men in polyester shirts stood out among those who were obviously reporters. A picture of Tony Soprano flashed through Sam's head.

She scanned the crowd for familiar faces, wondering if Pete Sanchez would station officers around the crowd because of the connection to Jake Calendar. She spotted a few business acquaintances and some of her customers.

A little rustle passed through the crowd, like aspen leaves on a windy day, and Sam looked to see that the stir originated near the front of the La Fonda. Tustin Deor's gelled hair showed above the little entourage that accompanied him and she caught a glimpse of his all-black clothing as he crossed the street. Evie Madsen clung to his arm, trying to stay up with his long stride in a pair of very awkward and clunky platform heels. He marched to the bandstand, paused and looked busy with his phone long enough to be sure that everyone within a block would notice him.

Evie with Tustin. Wow, that girl gets around, Sam thought, watching Evie give Tustin the same dewy eyed admiration that only days ago had been aimed at Jake Calendar. The girl's instant switch in affections could explain why she wasn't registered at the hotel. She'd merely moved in with a different guy. Tustin walked up the steps, flanked by Evie and the young gofer Sam had seen with him earlier at the bakery. They stood by the chairs at the table on stage. Another man quickly followed, apparently someone tied to a local radio station—he had that sort of voice—who stood by Tustin and greeted the crowd. They all smiled and waved, giving the audience time to ogle the star producer.

Eventually the murmur dwindled and Radio Voice introduced Tustin Deor with a flourish.

"Thank you. Thank you," he said, working to appear loveably humble yet great.

He read a thirty-second statement about how excited they were to be almost ready to launch season one of *You're The Star*, stating that auditions were already being organized in five major cities, and that the judges had been chosen. He announced each of the three personalities— with major pauses between—names that Sam had no clue about. She should have brought Kelly with her; that girl read *People* nearly every week.

Once he'd finished the dramatic announcement, Tustin opened it up for questions and the reporters surged forward. Sam realized that a lot of early publicity must have gone out to attract this crowd and this kind of excitement. No wonder Jake and Tustin were so desperate for the money to come in.

She spotted a uniformed officer at the edge of the crowd, one of Sanchez's men. Nearby, the chief himself watched, his thin lips a slash across the hard lines of his face, his coal black eyes barely moving. Like a feral cat, though, he probably saw everything.

Sam edged farther back in the crowd, getting a glance over the shoulder of a young female journalist who was reading down a list of pre-answered questions.

"One of your colleagues was killed a few days ago. What's happening with the investigation?" a reporter shouted from somewhere in the middle of the group.

Sam's neck-hairs prickled.

"We heard that a woman has been arrested," another man said.

Tustin Deor gave some platitudes—the old "we are assisting the local police in every way possible" kind of thing. A flat smile crossed Sanchez's face. Sam knew Deor's statement to be complete b.s., since he'd only been in town less than a day and had been standing in her bakery this very morning asking for money. Nonetheless, she didn't want to hang out until Sanchez noticed her and someone put it together. She backed to the edge of the gathering. Near the entrance to the La Fonda, half a block away, she spotted Vic Valentino. She hoped he hadn't seen her. The two mobster types were nowhere to be seen now.

She turned and ducked into one of the narrow alleyways that would take her out to the street and the safety of her shop. No way could she afford for one of those reporters to connect Sweet's Sweets to this awful thing and broadcast it with their usual endless speculation.

In the kitchen she called a quick meeting.

"If *anyone* comes in here asking about me, just say that I'm out. If they mention Jake Calendar's name, you know nothing. Don't even admit that he ever came in here—nothing." She glanced at Jen. "I have faith in you, hon. Be my gatekeeper."

"I can do it."

Julio spoke up. "I can get some guys. Like, if you want a security team."

"Uh, that's okay. Thank you, but I'm sure I'll be fine. I'm just going to get out and ask some questions. If it's urgent, call me. Otherwise, I don't plan on being either here or at home until all the reporters leave town."

Sam went out the back door, got in her truck and took off, unsure exactly what she would do the rest of the afternoon. She made a left and eased her way down Camino de la Placita, traffic from the press conference slowing things down. When she passed the side street where Beau's office was located she gazed toward it; a news van sat nearby. She cruised on.

Tom Calendar had said that Jake's desire was to become one of the elite Hollywood crowd. Sam wondered if she could find out whether he'd actually ever come close. He drove that expensive truck and dressed as a Tustin Deor lookalike. But that didn't mean anything. The vehicle could be financed for years to come and his clothes certainly weren't designer labels. He talked the talk—that might be the extent of his success.

She came to the entrance to Kit Carson Park where the lure of golden trees and shady walkways beckoned. She pulled the truck well away from view of the street, choosing a parking spot near the performing arts theater. With the windows down and the warm September air to calm her she began thinking of her list of suspects.

Evie, Tustin or one of his flunkies? Seeing those Vegas types at the news conference she was reminded of the hard-looking blond man who'd approached Jake near the plaza. Then there was still Vic Valentino, and there could also be someone else associated with the start-up production. Even Tom Calendar's face went through her mind. He seemed genuine enough, but Beau had taught her that no one could be above suspicion until the facts had ruled them out. She'd run through that much of the list when her phone rang.

"Hey, darlin' where are you?"

"The park. How about you?"

"I guess I just missed you at that press conference," he said. "I showed up about the time they started grilling him about Jake."

"I left about then. How did it go?"

"The entertainment news channels lost interest pretty quick. Jake's name must not be big news out there in California. The Albuquerque reporters got a little more mileage out of it. The Hollywood-underdog-gets-eaten-alive angle, questions that made it sound like Jake must have gotten involved in the show only to be dropped, his memory ignored, the minute he was gone."

"That could be pretty close to the truth. How did Deor handle those questions?"

"Went all solemn, worked up a couple tears, said his people wanted answers even more than the police did."

"Did he mention me?"

"Funny thing there. Somebody asked about the local woman they heard was arrested—Deor acted like he knew nothing about that."

"Maybe he hadn't heard."

"He's heard, if he's really working with the police as he claimed. My guess, he still wants money from you. Thinks maybe he can get it before you go on trial."

Well that was a happy thought.

Chapter 15

Sam closed her eyes and pictured the odd cast of characters in this whole thing. Evie Madsen's face kept coming up. She'd never actually talked with the girl but Evie had certainly given Sam the eye when she spoke to Jake. Jealousy? It was crazy to think that Jake would go back to his chubby, over-fifty ex when he had a girl like Evie. But crazy people were capable of doing crazy things.

Beau had said he was back at his office, doing some more background checks. At least he was accomplishing something. Sam's impatience rose; she felt like her life was on hold and there was nothing she could do about it. She put the truck in gear and drove back to her neighborhood.

A news van sat in front of Sweet's Sweets. Sam's gut

tightened. She could trust her crew not to talk; she wasn't sure she could trust herself not to rant about the injustice of it. Her attorney would have a fit if she appeared in front of a news camera. She kept rolling.

Surely these vultures would leave town soon and she could feel free to move about. She cruised past her old house, noting that it looked empty and quiet. She parked her truck around the corner and walked back, letting herself in the back door.

She turned on the computer. While it booted up she put the kettle on and found a mug and teabag.

With steaming mug beside her she sat at the desk, squared her shoulders and flexed her fingers. A quick visit to Netflix, where she searched Tustin Deor's name. Nothing. Wikipedia had a biography, which gave brief mention of one television production credit. The show sounded like a flash in the pan that aired six episodes before being canceled. She copied the name of the production company and pasted it into her browser, coming up with a glossy website that played up their single accomplishment as being far more successful than it was. Similarly, Tustin's personal website portrayed him as a cross between a corporate mogul and America's hottest bachelor.

On a whim, Sam ran a search on Evie Madsen. Several celebrity-watch websites appeared and she followed the link for the first one. Evie at the Oscars on the arm of a young man Sam didn't recognize; the caption with the picture associated him with one of the Batman movies. Then there was Evie at the Sundance Film Festival, Evie at the Grammys with some rapper, Evie at the Emmys—each time with a young man, each pose with sparkling eyes and a dazzling smile no doubt practiced in front of a mirror for maximum effect. Judging by the number of photos, either Evie was a lot more famous than Sam would have imagined or paparazzi would photograph anyone who happened to stand on a red carpet. She suspected the latter.

She slugged back the rest of her tea and turned the computer off, itchy to be moving again.

The street in front of Beau's office was clear of media vehicles so she parked down the block and walked there.

"Hey, I was just about to call you," he said, looking up from his keyboard. "Got some financial information on Tustin Deor."

She moved around to stand behind him and look at the screen.

"Credit rating—awful. Kelly's credit score is probably higher."

"Seriously? How can that be?"

"Looks like he had an influx of money a couple years ago."

"Which would jibe with what I found about his career—one production credit for a show that lasted less than a full season."

"Well, Tustin lives like that money came from a never-ending source. He ran through his entire cut from it within six months. Bought a big house, two cars and high-end furniture, all with minimums down and payments that stretch on for ages."

Just as Sam had suspected.

"Looks like he picks up the check for every party, stays at five-star hotels, the works. Travels all the time to stay ahead of the repo man and the bank. He's got fourteen credit cards, all maxed. Six months ago he began getting new cards to pay off old ones."

"I thought the banks had really cracked down on that stuff."

"Apparently not as much as you would imagine. He's got some of the cards in his own name, but a lot of them are under various business entities. Each time he has a brainstorm for a new project he forms a new company."

"My dad would call it robbing Peter to pay Paul."

"Exactly. There are also payments that don't match up with his known income, which tells me to look for a private source."

"So then . . . Would that be why he turned to Jake to help finance this *You're The Star* thing? Jake was every bit as flaky as Deor himself."

"*We* know that. But maybe Deor didn't." His fingers twitched near the keyboard.

"I saw two men at the press conference, Beau. Polyester shirts, hard faces—really didn't look like they were from around here. Did you see them?"

He shook his head. "Sound like the kind of men who would be willing to track down somebody who owed them money."

Loan sharks. Again, she remembered the man who'd come up to Jake on the street that evening outside the jewelry shop. He wasn't one of the men she'd seen at the press conference but something told her they were connected.

"Can we find out who they are?"

Beau nodded and made a note on a scrap of paper.

"Even if somebody like that came to town looking for Jake, it still doesn't really explain why they would kill Jake and try to frame me for it." Sam sat in one of the chairs across the desk from him. "And I don't see how Tustin benefits from Jake's death."

"Deor couldn't possibly have hoped to inherit from Jake, not unless he'd gotten him to write a will to that effect."

"Or to go in as a business partner? One of those deals where upon the death of one partner the other gets a big insurance policy or something?"

"He could have done that. He certainly had enough of these little business entities. Maybe he talked Jake into signing something." Beau tapped his index finger against the space bar on the keyboard, caught himself and quit. "Without getting into the corporate records in California, I don't know how we could find out. I'll try that track though—plus we still have the ex-wives and Jake's gambling to look into. What are you planning on next?"

She told him how Evie's involvement kept nagging at her and what she'd found when she researched the young woman.

"Clearly, she's got a good agent or a great dating service—showing up all the time with these various actors. I have to wonder why she showed up here in Taos with Jake. And now she's hanging on Tustin like a silk scarf. I'd like to ask her some questions," Sam said, "if I can ever catch her without Tustin attached at the hip."

"What time do your parents get back from Santa Fe?"

She glanced at her cell phone where the readout showed 4:37. "I better check in with Rupert. I asked him to entertain them as long as he could possibly handle their company." Her thank-you pastry for him would have to be something fabulous.

She scrolled through the numbers and pressed his. Rupert answered on the first ring and the conversation went quickly. She clicked off and looked at up Beau.

"They're just leaving Santa Fe. He said he couldn't talk them into staying there for dinner. He didn't sound all that unhappy to be bringing them back."

Beau smiled with good grace.

"So, I have maybe an hour," she said. "I wish we'd made more headway today. I want to get this solved and clear my name and get married so Mother and Daddy will go home."

Beau reached across the desk and took her hands. "We're doing what we can. More than Sanchez's department has done."

Sam squeezed his hands, then stood up. "I think I'll drop by the La Fonda and see if I can find Evie. Surely Tustin can't be in the room *all* the time."

At the hotel's front desk Sam wasn't surprised to find that they wouldn't give out Tustin Deor's room number. They did, however, agree to ring the room and ask if Ms. Madsen would accept the call. The clerk turned his back as the phone rang multiple times.

"Sorry, ma'am. No answer."

Sam debated leaving a message but didn't. She thanked the clerk and meandered toward the restaurant. As she passed the open doorway to the bar a flash of pink caught her eye. The light over the bar caught rosy liquid in crystal as the bartender set a glass down, and seated there accepting the drink was Evie. Once in awhile fortune does shine down, Sam thought. Evie was alone.

Sam edged up beside her and took the adjoining seat.

"Hi, Evie, how are you?"

Evie looked a little disconcerted but covered it by taking a long sip from her Cosmopolitan. She fixed her mouth in a sullen moue and regarded Sam through half-closed lids.

"Tustin's not with you?"

"He'll be down in a minute."

"I was surprised to see the two of you together. I mean, you seemed pretty infatuated with Jake just a few days ago."

"So?"

"I could understand what Jake saw in you—young and pretty and all. But I never quite got what you saw in him."

Evie sipped from the drink without responding.

"Did it bother you that Jake came to town to see me?"

Evie's eyes traveled from Sam's hair, which hadn't been combed since this morning, slowly downward to her day-glo green cross-trainers. A smug grin formed on the young woman's face.

"No, Sam, it didn't bother me at all."

Unless the girl was a far better actress than her

credentials suggested, there went Sam's theory that Evie's motive for striking out might have been jealousy. Still, it didn't explain why Evie suddenly showed up with a man so much older, when her normal taste went to the young and hip.

"What was Jake here for, really?" Sam leaned against the back of her barstool. The long day without answers was wearing her down.

Evie took another sip of the Cosmo. "Just what he told you, raising money to finance the show."

Sam searched her face for signs of deception but Evie had put on her clueless, Paris Hilton smile as she drained the rest of the drink. She started to get up but Sam placed a hand on her arm.

"When I didn't give Jake the money, was there trouble between him and Tustin? Or between you and Jake?"

Evie gave her a long stare, shook off the hand and walked out of the bar. Sam watched her head for the stairs. What was she so hostile about? Clearly, as she'd indicated, there was no reason to be jealous of Sam.

"Hot and cold, I'll tell you," said a male voice. The bartender. He held up a glass, asking with his eyes whether she wanted a drink.

She shook her head. "What do you mean, hot and cold?"

He tilted his head toward the doorway where Evie had just disappeared. "That one. Hot. You know what I mean . . . But *co-old*." He stretched out the word. "They've been here a few days. I've seen her pour herself all over a guy, you know, melting him. Then she's like she was just now. Won't give you the time of day."

"I suppose she gets a lot of unwanted attention, with looks like that."

He tipped his head. Maybe.

"She came in my shop a few days ago with a different guy, older man. Now she's with this young producer."

"Yeah, I noticed that too. The guy and her, they came in a few times on my shift."

"Did they have words? Some kind of argument?"

"The old guy or the young one?"

"Either."

He wiped at the bar, thinking. "Not really an argument. But something changed. She was all over the old guy the first day they checked in. The last time I saw them they were barely speaking. I guess that was Friday afternoon. She did that cold-shoulder thing and walked out, just like now."

"Do you remember anything else about that day?"

"He had a little bag with him, purple, paper sack."

Sam's breath caught.

"While I was making their drinks he opened the bag and made some kind of comment to the lady. Right after that is when Miss Cosmo got all huffy."

So maybe Evie *had* believed that Sam sent the cupcake as a gift for Jake. If she'd said that to the police, it could be the real basis for their case against Sam.

"Did you see where he got the bag? Did someone deliver it?"

The bartender shrugged. "I can't say. He had it with him when I first noticed it."

Jen had already told Sam that Jake hadn't bought anything at the bakery that day. She'd sold a dozen or more of the chocolate cupcakes but not to him.

"You could ask at the front desk," the bartender said. "The guy did act like it was something he'd received as a gift. Maybe somebody left it there for him."

"So the woman left first. Did you see where the man went? Did he leave the hotel or did he go up to their room?"

"I didn't see. Things got busy about that time and I never really noticed when he left."

She thanked him and pulled out some money, which he pushed back across the bar.

"I hope you get this resolved, Ms. Sweet."

Had he known who she was all along? She dug out a business card and asked him to give a call if he thought of anything else related to Jake Calendar or Evie Madsen.

Sam walked straight to the front desk, where she had to wait behind two other people who were checking in. When her turn came the young man in the white shirt and black tie turned a polite smile her way.

"Checking in?"

"No, actually I had a question about a gift that might have been delivered here Friday afternoon. A small, purple paper sack. Were you here at the time?"

He looked at the ceiling, thinking. "Yeah . . . I remember it. I gave it to the guest, name Challenger or something like that."

"Calendar. That's right. Can you tell me who delivered the gift in the first place?"

He shook his head slowly. "It was already here when I came on duty. Sitting back there on that counter. Celina, who works the desk until three, told me to be sure to stop Mr. Calendar if I saw him and give him the bag."

Sam got the coworker's name but he wouldn't give out her number. She thanked him and stepped out to the sidewalk, dialing Beau's cell.

"I need to reach a Celina Romero who works as a desk clerk at the La Fonda."

He didn't question, just tapped into one of his databases. "There are three Celina Romeros in the DMV records. One is aged seventy-eight, so that's probably not the one." He gave addresses of the other two. "Do not ever tell anyone how you got that information unless you want to see me lose my job."

"Don't worry. I've got a pretty good idea which one it is and I just have one or two questions for her."

When her friend at the hotel desk talked about his coworker, Sam had the impression she was younger so she headed for the home of the Celina who was only twenty-five. The flat-roofed house was in an older neighborhood and when a woman in her fifties answered the door Sam realized that Celina lived with her parents.

"She went to the market for me," the elder Mrs. Romero said. "She should be home soon."

"If it's okay, I'll wait for her. I can sit out here in my truck."

"No, no, come on inside. I know you," Mrs. Romero said. "You're the bakery lady. I see your van driving around town sometimes, and my grandchildren love to come by for cookies after school."

She ushered Sam into a cube of a living room, filled with seventies furniture and a little shrine of the Virgin Mary against one wall. The smell of pinto beans reminded Sam that her parents would be arriving soon and she had absolutely no idea what she was feeding them for dinner. Hopefully, Rupert had gotten them a big lunch.

"I need to check my tortillas," Mrs. Romero said, leaving through a doorway where Sam could see a table with three place settings.

Sam glanced anxiously at the digital clock numerals on a DVD player beneath the television set. Rupert could be pulling into town any minute. She gave Beau a quick call and asked if he would be home to let them in.

Celina Romero came through the door just then, startled to see a stranger sitting on the avocado green sofa. Sam stood up, introduced herself and quickly posed her question.

"I remember the purple bag. There was a note with his name on it clipped to the front." And although she described Evie Madsen to a T, Celina couldn't remember if Evie brought the bag or if she simply remembered Evie because she'd been staying with Jake.

Sam left with one important fact stuck in her head. The police hadn't mentioned a note.

Chapter 16

Speeding along the back roads of town, talking on her cell phone wasn't a great idea. Sam knew this. But the revelation of the existence of a note with the poisoned cupcake was crucial. The handwriting on the note could prove that Sam didn't send it. She reached Mark Nelson just as he was leaving his office.

"Among the evidence the police showed to you, was there a note with Jake Calendar's name on it? A note that would have been attached to that bakery bag." She quickly explained what she'd just learned from the hotel staff.

"I didn't see one," he said. "It sure doesn't show up in the photograph of the evidence bag that contains the purple sack. And it's not listed as a separate item on the evidence list."

"They can't withhold that from us, can they?"

"No, they have to disclose it. I'll get on this first thing in the morning."

She must have let out a little whine.

"Sam, I would do it now but I'm already late for a Rotary meeting where I'm the keynote speaker. Another night won't hurt and I promise I won't forget."

One look at the note, one sample of her own handwriting, and the prosecutors would have a very hard time making their case, but she quelled her impatience. What choice did she have? She headed toward home and when she pulled in at the big gate saw Rupert's Land Rover parked in her usual spot, with Beau's Explorer nearby.

The smell of chicken and biscuits greeted her when she walked in. *Beau, I love you, I love you.*

"Thought cooking tonight would be a strain," he said when she hugged him.

Her father was stretched back in the recliner, his nightly bourbon at hand, and Rupert was sniffing around the big deli box of fried chicken. It wasn't terribly difficult to persuade him to stay.

"Where have you been all day, Samantha Jane? You missed a beautiful day in Santa Fe." Nina Rae held up an exquisitely woven shawl she must have purchased.

Sam gave her mother a look. *Trying to clear myself of a murder charge seemed a little more important than shopping . . .* But she put on her smile and announced brightly that dinner was on the table.

Rupert and Howard filled plates with chicken, coleslaw, three-bean salad and green salad. Beau saw to it that everyone's drink glasses were filled, while Sam poured herself a half-glass of wine and sat beside the fireplace for a minute to unwind. When the others had settled around the table she joined them, picking the crispy coating off her chicken breast and dribbling only a few drops of dressing over her little pile of lettuce and tomato. That dress would still fit, no matter how long this investigation went on.

The thought that it might take weeks to clear her name left Sam feeling deflated. She looked around the table—picturing her parents staying on forever, having to call on friends like Rupert to run interference, she and Beau simply wanting to start married life and get away on their trip, all while it felt like they weren't gaining much in the way of evidence to free her—she felt her energy drain away.

"Not hungry?" Beau whispered beside her. "I could get you something else."

She squeezed his hand under the table. "No, I'll be fine."

The evening dragged by, with Rupert making a quick exit when they started another domino game suggested by Nina Rae. Finally, Sam left the elder Sweets to their late television news program and went upstairs for a shower and her favorite snuggly nightgown. Beau was waiting in bed when she came out of the bathroom.

"Are you sure you're doing okay?" he asked as she slid under the covers.

"Sorry, it's just a mood. I'm impatient to be done with this whole police thing that has messed up all our plans."

"Want to brainstorm a little?" He put an arm around

her shoulders. "Did you ever contact that Celina Romero whose address I looked up for you?"

Her mood lightened a little. She sat upright, facing him.

"Actually, yes. I don't know how this will play out but she said there was a note clipped to the bakery bag that held the cupcake. After I spoke to Celina I talked to Mark Nelson and asked him to review the evidence the police showed him. If that note is in there, it will be someone else's handwriting. That fact alone could clear me."

"It would go a long way," he said.

"But what if the note isn't there? I'm worried that it could have been lost anywhere along the way. Jake might have tossed it in the trash."

"Police would have taken the contents of the room's waste baskets."

But there were other places, Sam thought. The bar, the lobby, some ashtray in the hall. She pulled herself away from that train of thought. No point envisioning how easily the note could have vanished.

"What if the police are withholding that evidence, not including it with the information they gave Mark?"

"Eventually, it would have to come out. It would take a very crooked cop with a personal vendetta to risk tampering like that."

She met his gaze. The chief himself didn't like Beau. But was that reason enough to sabotage an investigation in order to harm Sam? Surely not.

"I'll ask my contact over at the PD to poke around and see what he can find. If that note was logged into evidence you have a right to see it."

"I'll give a handwriting sample. It'll be easy to prove I didn't write it."

"Don't volunteer too much too soon. Let's see what they have first."

It was probably exactly what Mark Nelson would say, too.

"What if Evie is involved in this? According to the bartender they were together just before going up to their room, and from the police timeline we know that he died within an hour after that."

"What's her motive? To do this over an old girlfriend he hadn't seen in thirty years, who was about to marry another man? Seems pretty extreme."

"Think how young Evie is. Kids these days take extreme measures. Look at a guy who'll pick up a gun and take out a bunch of strangers just because he's had a rough time of it at school."

"True. And it's true that poisoning is typically more of a woman's method for killing. Less confrontational." He leaned back against the headboard. "Maybe we need to look at women with closer connections to Jake."

"Jake mentioned being married. Maybe Tom Calendar can give us more information, like names. We could check out the ex-wives." She reached for her phone. "It's an hour earlier in California—let me see if I can reach him."

Tom's phone went to an answering machine and Sam left both her own and Beau's numbers.

"I don't know . . ." she said after setting the phone aside. "Women might be poisoners but it seems a little farfetched that an ex-wife would go to these lengths."

And maybe that was another reason the police had homed in on Sam. She found her thoughts taking a circular route as she snuggled next to Beau and he turned out the lamp. When he began trailing little kisses along her neck and earlobe the problems sort of disappeared quickly.

By daylight Sam was wide awake again, myriad thoughts coming at her like arrows at a target. She eased out of bed to let Beau sleep a little longer, showered, dressed in jeans and a favorite shirt. On her side of the bathroom vanity the wooden box looked up at her, perhaps a bit ignored in recent days.

"You can help me," she said, instantly chiding herself for talking to a hunk of wood.

She picked it up and held it close. The familiar warm glow spread from her hands to her arms and soon energized her whole body. She set it down and opened the lid to choose a pair of beaded earrings.

"That thing looks different," Beau said in a fuzzy voice, walking in wearing pajama bottoms and a sleepy face.

Sam glanced at the box. The quilt-patterned carving indeed retained some of the golden glow it always got when she held it. Although Beau knew of her experiences with the box's power, he'd never actually witnessed it in action. She decided this wasn't the time for a demo.

"I dusted it yesterday," she said.

"You look so beautiful this morning, darlin'." He wound his arms around her waist and nuzzled her hair.

"Want to come back to bed?"

Another effect of the box's magic—Sam's allure seemed to increase when she'd held it. How tempting to simply crawl back under the covers, pretend they were already on their honeymoon, ignore both her parents and the entire overriding problem with the police. He saw the flicker of emotions cross her face.

"I know," he said. "More important things to do today."

"*Never* more important—just necessary. Like solving this whole stupid mess so we *really* can enjoy ourselves."

He gave her a squeeze and turned on the shower. She blew him a kiss and left the room before the sight of him peeling off those pajamas could make her change her mind.

Her parents' bedroom door was closed, no strip of light showing at the bottom, so Sam tiptoed to the kitchen where she started coffee. Gathering her pack and jacket she let herself out and got into her truck. It wasn't yet eight o'clock but she took a chance and dialed Mark Nelson's office. The recorded message informed her that office hours were nine to five. Still, he might be there, working before the receptionist came in. She decided to take the chance and drop by.

A white Cadillac Escalade was parked at the side of the building. But the door was locked and he didn't respond to a knock or to a tap at one of the side windows. When she dialed his cell phone it, too, went to voicemail. She suppressed a surge of impatience. The man probably just needed time to work in peace. If Mark had answers he would let her know.

She turned around and headed for her old house, where she caught Kelly in an oversized T-shirt, pouring what was obviously her first cup of coffee for the day.

"Hey there," Sam said in her most wheedling voice. "Do you suppose Riki would let you take the day off? Or at least half of it?"

Kelly paused with the cup at her lips, sending Sam a half-lidded stare.

"I need someone to be entertainment chairperson for your grandparents today. I really have to be here, working with Beau to find answers and clear my name, and it's hard to keep them from being bored."

"Sure—I'd like to spend some more time with them anyway. I'll try to beg at least a partial day. How am I going to keep them busy?"

"Well, I thought you might do the Enchanted Circle drive. You know, Angel Fire, Eagle Nest, Red River and back. Lots of shopping to keep your grandmother happy, lots of nice lunch places along the way . . ." The route, which circled New Mexico's highest mountain was roughly a hundred miles of breathtaking scenery, punctuated by picturesque little ski towns.

Kelly brightened further when Sam pulled cash out of her wallet. Sam could read her thoughts—getting out sure beat playing endless domino games at the dining table.

"Just don't drive a million miles an hour. We want them to spend a day having fun, not spend it throwing up on those curving mountain roads."

"I can handle it." Kelly took a long slug of her coffee and picked up the phone to talk to her boss.

"Call your grandmother in another hour or so and tell her when you'll pick them up."

One down, a hundred to go on the to-do list, Sam thought as she left.

She drove toward the plaza, Evie Madsen's face pestering her, as it had all night. No matter what Beau said, Sam couldn't help but think of the girl's cold manner. Maybe she saw Tustin as the bigger fish and getting rid of Jake seemed like a solution; Tustin after all appeared to have lots of money and maybe he treated her well.

Maybe Jake had become jealous and they'd argued. The fact that Jake had flirted with Sam when he came to town could have made Evie's twisted little mind decide that Sam could be made to look guilty in the process. But killing? Evie dumped men all the time. The vengeance line of thinking was very junior-high—but then Evie didn't seem much brighter than the average thirteen year old.

Sam drummed her nails on the steering wheel as she sat at a red light. Confronting Evie at the hotel hadn't worked too well yesterday. She would have to come up with something better. Probably not a gift from Sweet's Sweets though. A horn tooted behind her and she realized the light had turned green. She turned left, skirting the outer edge of the plaza trying to decide whether to stop in at her shop or what, exactly, her next move should be. The same beeping horn sounded behind her again.

What was this guy's problem? She couldn't exactly run down the car ahead just to please someone who was late for work. She glanced back in her mirror. It was a red BMW and it looked like Tustin Deor at the wheel. She drove through the narrow section of street where two-way traffic was hemmed in by close curbs on both sides. A block later, the road widened slightly and she edged to the right. Instead of passing, Tustin followed.

Fine. I wanted to talk to you anyway.

She made a right turn and pulled into the wide parking lot of a consignment shop. The Beemer came alongside and Tustin jumped out before she'd even powered down her window. The young flunky with the cell phone waited in the car, chatting away with someone.

"Samantha, I'm glad I saw you back there," Tustin said, flashing that people-charmer smile. "I was planning to stop by your shop."

His gelled hair stood up and in the sunlight she saw that he had tiny freckles on his forehead. It gave him a farm kid look, like he could be Tom Sawyer's crony.

"I guess I owe you a debt of thanks," she said. "For not pointing me out in the crowd yesterday at the news conference."

"No problem." He glanced off to the west for a second. "Look, the real reason I wanted to chat with you was to see if I couldn't change your mind about investing with us. Could we do lunch? Pick a nice place."

"I've really got a full day," she said, although she wouldn't mind asking him a few more questions about Evie. Although he hadn't been in town at the time he might know how the young woman had spent last Friday afternoon. The turn-off was the idea of spending an hour with someone whose only goal was to talk her out of money—kind of like those way-too-friendly timeshare presentations.

He rested a forearm on the edge of her window. "Jake thought very highly of you, Sam. This isn't about the size of the investment, is it? Because Jake said you'd done really well for yourself, selling that Cantone sketchbook for—well, I have no idea but I heard rumor that it was six or seven figures."

"I can't invest with you, Tustin."

"But Jake said—"

"Even if I had the money, which I don't, I wouldn't. It seems like a very speculative investment."

His eyes narrowed, his face hardening. "That could prove to be a very bad decision."

"Is that a threat?" She edged her hand toward the window buttons.

His smile reappeared. "Not at all. I just think when the show hits number one in the ratings you'll wish you'd gotten in on it. It'll be an excellent return on your money."

Chapter 17

She watched Deor saunter back to the BMW and climb in, acting like he owned the world. She wondered how many thousands were still due on the car, let alone his other massive debts. It was amazing how people began to believe their own images.

He started the car and roared out of the parking lot, narrowly missing a UPS truck. She held her breath as the driver slammed on his brakes and glared at the red car.

Her phone rang and she picked it up. Beau.

"Hey, darlin', how's the search going?"

"Well, I just blew a chance to ask some more questions about Evie's whereabouts on Friday," she said, telling him about the encounter with Tustin. "Why? Do you have any news?"

"I contacted my friend in the police department and asked him to check on the note that was with the cupcake bag. Haven't heard anything yet. Kelly called your mother and said she would come out to the house and take them out for the day."

"I know. Thank goodness for everybody who's pitching in this week. I'm feeling a little let down that we haven't been able to get more information."

"Would it help if I went by the hotel and talked to Evie?" he asked. "She might feel like she has to answer questions if they come from someone in uniform. She won't know that this isn't my case."

"Good idea. You might be able to get more out of the hotel staff too. In the meantime, what can I be working on? I really feel at loose ends."

"Hang in there. We'll start getting answers soon. I'll call you when I come up with something."

She hoped those answers came *very* soon. Waiting to hear from her attorney, waiting for Beau's contact in the police department and waiting to see what Evie had to say—all this spare energy with no outlet for it was driving her crazy. She started her truck and rolled out of the lot, covering the few blocks to Sweet's Sweets.

"What are you doing here?" Becky asked, looking up from a child's birthday cake with a brown sugar stretch of beach and a gray candy shark roaring up out of blue-gel icing.

"I can't stand sitting around and hoping the police or my attorney come up with answers. I have to be doing something." Sam pulled on a baker's jacket and turned to Julio. "Do you have any cookies I can decorate or something?"

Within fifteen minutes Sam had decorated six dozen butter cookies. Normally after handling the wooden box her energy level went a little ballistic and she could accomplish an amazing amount of work in a short time. But she always did this little feat at night when the employees weren't around to witness. She told herself to slow down.

She carried the tray of cookies out front for the display, took a deep breath and went back to see what else awaited. She was nearly finished with the three dozen fancy cupcakes they would need for the afternoon crowd when Beau called.

"I'm at the La Fonda," he said, "and I got access to the room where Jake stayed. No other guests have used it yet and it hasn't been cleaned. I thought you and I might conduct a little investigation of our own."

"Is this going to get you in trouble?"

"The police released the crime scene, so it's up to the hotel manager how soon he wants to put it back in use. I just asked him to hold off a little longer."

"I'll be there in ten minutes."

She washed her hands, switched the baker's jacket for her regular shirt again, and headed out the front door. It would be simpler to walk the two blocks than to find parking on the plaza in the middle of a busy morning. She found Beau in Room 301, where he'd told her to come.

"Put these on," he said, handing over a pair of latex

gloves. "Even though they released the room, the police could always come back and it wouldn't be good for our prints to be here."

She scanned the room—typical setup with king-sized bed, two nightstands, a pine desk with a cute-but-uncomfortable looking iron-backed chair, and a pine armoire. Indian blanket motif bedding added to the Southwestern feel, and a kiva fireplace in one corner gave a touch of coziness. Three windows overlooked the plaza and a door led to a balcony.

"This one adjoins room 302," Beau said with a tilt of his head, "and they share the balcony, but someone else was staying in that one and all the connecting doors were locked the whole time, according to the manager."

Chocolate crumbs littered a corner of the desk; no one had bothered to brush them into the trash basket below and the receptacle was completely empty.

"Look around for the note that the desk clerk said was attached to the bakery bag," she said, lifting the skirting around the bed. "Just in case."

"Bathroom's empty," he called out. "I guess the police took what they wanted and tossed any personal possessions into the suitcase that Tom Calendar took home with him."

The bed was one of those built on a solid wooden base and there was little chance that an item would end up between it and the bed skirt but Sam crawled on hands and knees all the way around, making sure. No sign of the note. When she stood up her vision blurred and she squeezed her eyes shut. Opening them, she saw a vague grayish form near the desk, almost human in shape. It bent over the corner where the cupcake crumbs were scattered. She strained to recognize it but the vision dissipated and vanished.

"B—" she started to call out. But what was there to say?

Her hands tingled faintly, reminding her that she'd handled the wooden box this morning. Similar things had happened before—colored auras, glowing fingerprints invisible to the naked eye. It was downright spooky and she knew from experience that other people couldn't see them. She walked to the desk and stared hard but no prints appeared to her, no trace of the ghostly figure.

"Sam? What's the matter?" Beau had come out of the bathroom and was staring at her face. "You're awfully pale."

She blinked again. "Really? I guess I stood up too fast. I thought I saw some—" She shook her head. "Never mind. It probably wasn't anything."

Nothing but an overactive imagination, she told herself. She crossed over to the small rounded fireplace and looked at the arrangement of ceramic logs stacked to look like a pile of wood. Beneath them, the crumbly fake ashes looked normal enough. She stooped down and poked her gloved finger through them—no burned scraps of paper. Where was that note?

Beau had walked out to the balcony and when Sam stood and turned toward the center of the room it happened again. A grey figure near the desk, but this one was slightly different from the first—taller, broader in the shoulders.

"Beau, can you come here?" she said without taking her eyes off the faint shape.

She heard his tread crossing the balcony, stepping through the doorway.

"Do you see anything over by the desk?"

"On the floor? Or on the desk itself?"

The shape melted away. Clearly, he hadn't seen it.

"No, it's gone now. I just thought I saw something." Was this another aura-like vision, or did she want answers so badly that she was fooling herself into seeing them?

"Well, I don't see anything useful here," Beau said, closing the balcony door and locking it. "Looks like the police took everything that might have helped us."

Sam stripped off her gloves and handed them over to him, disappointed.

"Well, there's still hope that the police do have the note and that Mark Nelson can get a copy of it."

They stepped out into the corridor and Beau locked the room. He slipped an arm around her shoulders as they walked toward the stairs.

"There's also a chance that the killer got hold of the note and destroyed it after Jake got the package," he said. "You need to be prepared for the idea that it may never turn up."

"So, who had access to Jake's room other than Evie? You're not suggesting the hotel personnel?"

"Mr. Deor, the fancy-schmancy producer?"

"No. He arrived in town after Jake died so he could take over the press conference. That, and pestering me for money."

"Well, there are lots of ways to get into hotel rooms. We really can't rule out anyone."

A picture of Vic Valentino, the unfortunate singer who'd failed so miserably at his audition attempt, came into her head. She thought about him as she and Beau walked through the lobby. Valentino, aka Victor Garcia, was slightly built. So was the first of the two smoke-like apparitions she'd seen in the room. Valentino also had a reason to hate Jake Calendar. Perhaps he'd thought with Jake out of the way that he could get to someone higher up with *You're The Star* and manage to get a more successful audition with somebody else—he'd almost admitted that to Sam when she'd visited his home. Maybe they should talk to him again. She said as much to Beau when they reached the sidewalk.

"Could you question him this time?" she suggested. "I didn't get much out of him. Meanwhile, I want to run by Mark Nelson's office and see what he may have found out about the note."

They parted ways outside the hotel. As she walked back toward her shop Sam found herself thinking about the two visions she'd had in Jake's room. They weren't well defined, not clearly human beings, but they certainly didn't look animal or ghostly in the Casper sense. They were almost more like energy fields. Still, she had to wonder, had she just witnessed the figure of the person who poisoned the cupcake?

She retrieved her truck from the alley where she'd parked it, cranked the engine and headed out to see her attorney.

The law offices looked moderately busy from the outside. Five vehicles, including the Escalade Mark Nelson drove. She went inside, hoping she wouldn't get the runaround or have to wait through someone else's long consultation. Luckily, he was standing at the reception desk and there was no graceful way for him to escape. He invited her into the conference room and closed the door.

"No luck, Sam. I'm sorry. The note didn't show up in any of the photos or on the evidence list, so I went by the police station. They swear they never found a note at the scene."

Her mood plummeted. Life would have become a whole lot simpler with that bit of evidence. Nelson didn't have anything to help lighten her spirit so she left, wondering just how helpful he really wanted to be. He would certainly bill a lot more hours if this thing went all the way to trial. She and Beau needed to find answers, quickly.

Her phone rang as she was getting into her truck.

"Another lead," Beau said.

At this point almost any news had to be positive.

"I got a callback from Tom Calendar and he gave me the names of Jake's former wives. Did you know there were three? So, anyway, I made a call to Vital Statistics in Sacramento. No info on the first one—Tom said it was twenty-five years ago and they divorced a year later in Nevada—but the other two took place in California. Wife number two was Glenda Tronto. That lasted seven years—maybe someone got the itch."

"All that sounds like way old history," Sam said, wondering where this was going.

"It's the last one that gets interesting. Six years ago he married Doralee Wickham. Tom said they had their problems but wasn't sure whether they'd officially split. The court records show that Jake filed for divorce in May of this year. The records don't show whether it became final. I requested information on the couple's finances but haven't gotten anything back on that."

"That's recent enough that a scorned woman might still be angry enough to retaliate," Sam mused.

"That's only one half of the news," Beau said. "Each week I review the county traffic citations—checking to see if any new warrants might have been issued against someone we've had contact with—and I remembered yesterday seeing a female driver from California listed, speeding through the red light at the ski valley road—"

"Beau! Bottom line."

"Doralee Wickham Calendar."

"Jake's most recent ex was here, in Taos County."

"Yes. She got the ticket four days ago."

"What would she be doing here unless it had something to do with Jake?"

"Exactly."

Sam chewed at her lower lip. "I wonder how we might track her down and find out what was going on."

"I was getting to that. She registered at the Taos Inn."

"I need to talk to her," Sam said, turning the ignition on the truck and putting it in gear. "Do you know her room number?"

"Sam, slow down," he said. "We don't even know if she's still in town. She gave that as her local address when she got the ticket."

"Still . . . it wouldn't hurt to check. And I can ask questions that your deputies wouldn't, like whether she and Jake were legally divorced yet."

Obviously, Beau realized there was no use arguing with her. He wished her luck. She arrived at the Taos Inn, pulling into the crowded parking lot with its overhang of green, copper and golden cottonwood leaves. A rippling breeze caught them as Sam locked her truck and headed for the lobby.

She picked up a house phone and asked to be connected and was almost surprised to find Doralee in her room and agreeable to a meeting. Five minutes later the woman entered the spacious lobby from one of the side corridors. She might have been a carbon copy of Sam fifteen years younger, with more brown in her hair than grey at this point and a dozen pounds lighter. She wore a blouse printed with emerald green geometric patterns, a dark brown skirt and a pair of brown pumps. It was something Sam might have chosen for herself at an earlier age. Doralee eyed Sam as if she were seeing her older self.

"I couldn't believe it about Jake," Doralee said once they'd settled into a pair of heavily carved Mexican chairs at one end of the huge room. "I've just been sitting in my room, thinking I should go claim his things."

"You weren't divorced?" Sam didn't mention that Jake's brother had already done the claiming. It would be interesting to see where Doralee was going with this.

"Sadly, we were in the process. I . . . well, I think Jake had found someone else. For awhile I thought it might be you. It's why I came to Taos. To see what you were like. 'Samantha Sweet, Sam this and Sam that' . . . he talked about you a lot. I had to think maybe . . ." She rubbed the palms of her hands along the chair's arms. "After a day or two I realized you weren't the threat. His big interest was obviously in that *teenager* who was hanging on his arm."

"You mean you saw me before today?"

"At your bakery. I knew the name of the place. Jake had jotted it on a note at home. I knew the young lady at the front counter couldn't be you, but when you walked out front once, wearing a white jacket, I knew that had to be you."

Doralee was *watching* her? Okay, that was a little creepy.

"But then I caught sight of Jake with Little Miss Cutie in Pink."

"So, you came all the way to Taos to get a look at whoever Jake was leaving you for?"

Doralee nodded. "I had to know." She pinched the fabric of her skirt into pleats, working them with her fingers but the instant she let go the material fell back into its original smooth shape.

"It's hard being the third wife, you know. You're never sure why those earlier tries didn't work—did they leave him, did he leave them, was it always for a younger woman?"

Was it because you're so insecure that you drove him nuts?

"Did you actually speak to Jake, here in town?"

Doralee gave up on pleating the skirt and began picking at her cuticles. "I tried to. Thursday evening he and *Pinky* were having drinks at some little bar about a block away from the plaza. I saw them go in there and I wanted a public place to talk to him, you know, so he couldn't ignore me. I took the divorce papers he'd already signed and asked him to tear them up so we could get back together."

Sam could only imagine how well Jake would appreciate that.

"He got real mad at me, and it became sort of a scene. When the cops came I just left."

Cops?

"I never saw him again." The voice went soft and Doralee's eyes got moist. "I can't tell you much more than that."

Doralee stood up and had disappeared down the corridor before Sam could think what else to ask her.

Sam went out to her truck. A scene where the police were called? There had to be a record of it. A mere argument wouldn't bring the cops; there had to be more to the story.

Sam left the Taos Inn, realizing that it was nearly two o'clock and she'd never eaten any lunch. She was debating whether to succumb to the call of fast food or go home for something or try to skip eating until this evening. About the time she drove past McDonald's with that irresistible scent of French fries wafting through the air her phone rang.

"Mom, oh my god, I don't know what to do!" Kelly's

voice went high and squeaky, near panic.

A million thoughts went through Sam's head. Her parents, a wreck, some road emergency. "What happened, Kel? Slow down."

"I can't believe— It's a mess. My stuff."

"Kelly, breathe."

Sam heard a deep breath on the line. "Someone broke into the house."

Chapter 18

Sam whipped the truck into a U turn at the first possible chance and arrived at her house minutes later. Kelly stood beside her car in the driveway and rushed into Sam's arms as soon as the red pickup came to a halt.

"They aren't still in there, are they?" Sam asked, one eye on the back door.

"No. I'm pretty sure not. It just shocked me to walk in there. I don't want to go in by myself."

"I've called Beau and he's—" His cruiser's siren finished the statement.

With a hand on his holster he told the two women to wait outside. He came back two minutes later saying it was okay to come in.

From the moment they stepped through the back

door they faced chaos. In the kitchen drawers had been dumped, strewing cutlery and knives across the counter tops. Food packages were opened, leaving cereal and crackers and coffee and sugar in a crunchy, sticky mess on the floor and across the implements on the work surfaces.

"This is unreal," Sam said. "More like vandalism than a robbery."

Beau came in from the living room. "Oh it was a robbery too. Your computer is gone."

Sam had taken her new laptop to Beau's, leaving the older desktop model for Kelly. She tried to think what might be on it. Basically, everything.

"Did you have it password protected?" Beau asked.

"Yes. At least that will stop them."

"Slow them down. Anyone who really wants the information can find somebody with the skills to hack into it. If you ever did any banking or shopping on there, you'll want to change all your accounts right away."

Sam followed him to the desk in the corner of the room. Papers lay everywhere but she found the little flowered diary where she'd written her various passwords in her own coded system so that they looked like addresses and phone numbers. She grabbed it up and put it in her pocket.

"Kelly, where are your grandparents? Did they see this?"

"Fortunately, no. I took them by Beau's after we finished our drive. Grampa looked like he wanted a nap."

Thank goodness. Sam didn't need to try explaining to her parents that Kelly would be perfectly safe. She wasn't all that sure of it herself.

"Here's where they got in," Beau said, showing her that the small side window by the front door had been smashed in. "They reached in and twisted open the deadbolt. I'll get someone out to repair it and change the locks."

"I can do the locks," Sam said. "I've got spares out in the truck." Knowing how to break into places had taught her a few valuable skills.

"Oh, god," Kelly wailed from a distance.

Sam followed her daughter's voice and found Kelly in her own bedroom. The mattress lay halfway across the room, where someone had upended it to look under. In the process it had crashed into her dresser top and broken two bottles of perfume, which saturated the carpet and bedding. The room smelled like an intense flower garden.

"That was my favorite," Kelly said as she picked up the crystal heart-shaped top to one of the bottles.

"You can get new ones. I'm sure our insurance will cover a lot of this."

Sam rushed across the hall to her old room. Her heart raced. In here the mattress had been slashed and stuffing lay in tufts like a big indoor snowstorm. All the empty dresser drawers gaped open at odd angles. The few things she'd left in the closet lay in heaps on the floor; someone had obviously gone through pockets and then tossed them aside. Her wedding gown looked as if it had been trampled. Sam fell to her knees and gently scooped it up. Shaking it carefully she saw that it appeared intact, only wrinkled. She reached for the padded hanger to re-hang it.

"The bathroom too," Kelly called out.

"Don't start cleaning things up," Beau cautioned. "You'll need to file a police report."

"I don't want anything to do with them," Sam said. Pete Sanchez had already ruined her week.

"Your insurance will require it. Kelly could make the call."

They stood in the relatively unharmed dining room while Kelly spoke to someone who was obviously asking whether she was in danger at the moment, were the burglars still on the premises and other things that seemed designed to waste time when someone could be on the way. Finally, Beau got on the phone and threw a few cop-code numbers at the dispatcher and was told an officer would be there soon.

Soon turned out to be forty minutes but it was better than nothing. Beau met the police officer—luckily, not one that Sam knew—and walked him through the house telling him what they'd noticed was missing at first glance. Meanwhile, Kelly had the presence of mind to walk around snapping pictures with her phone. Sam leaned one hip against the dining table, her foot tapping and her mind going a thousand directions. This was no random grab-a-TV burglary; they had been after something specific. People don't slash mattresses and dump cereal boxes unless they've got some time and are searching. But for what?

Money? Did Tustin Deor really believe what Jake had told him—that Sam had a lot of ready cash? Could he have possibly done this? Even if she'd agreed to invest in his project, did he honestly think she kept cash in the mattress? All her files and banking paperwork were at Beau's now, but she thought of the missing computer. She would have to take care of that as soon as possible.

She pictured Deor in his thousand dollar wristwatch and designer jeans with that prissy little short jacket he wore. Ripping and digging through drawers hardly seemed his style. Still, you never knew. He did have his little entourage with him and that one big guy could bully his way through a brick wall, she'd bet. She mentioned it to Beau while the officer got information from Kelly.

"This has to be aimed at me," Sam said in a low voice. "This address is under my name in the phone book. It's where anyone who doesn't know me very well would naturally come looking."

"You think that Hollywood guy came out here?"

She shrugged. "I don't know. He certainly got pushy about the money he thought I should give him. But a lot of people connected me with Jake. Doralee Calendar could have come looking for something, although if she did she was certainly cool about it an hour ago. Maybe those rough guys that Jake owed money to . . ."

Beau bit at the corner of his lip. "This seems extreme but I'll check it out."

He stood in the corner of the kitchen and quietly made a few phone calls. When he looked up the uniformed officer was finishing his report.

"I'll have this typed and you can pick up a copy anytime after tomorrow morning," he told Kelly and Sam. He walked out to his cruiser and drove away.

"Tustin Deor is still registered at the La Fonda," Beau said, "but no one answers in the room. I've got my men watching out for his car. If we can pull him over we might get the chance to talk to him. That's about all I can do for now so I guess I'll head home."

"See you there," Sam said. "Can you see that my folks get their usual happy hour treats? I'll be along after I help Kelly with this mess. When we get a chance to talk I've got more."

"It's all right, Mom. You don't have to hang out here. I can clean up. I wasn't doing much tonight anyway."

Sam stayed long enough to find a board in the garage and nail it over the broken window and assure that the deadbolt locks were functioning. They closed the door on Sam's old room with the shredded mattress—it could wait until later—and put Kelly's bed back together. Sam's earlier energy came in handy as she organized the kitchen while Kelly worked in the living room.

"I don't want you here alone tonight," Sam told her. "If you can't find a friend to come stay with you, at least come out and take the couch at our place."

"Thought of that already. Jen's free and she'll come by right after work."

Sam placed a kiss in the center of Kelly's forehead. "Take care of yourselves. Don't open the door to anyone, and call Beau the instant you hear any strange noise."

Kelly gave a brave smile. "We'll be fine."

But the break-in kept nagging at Sam all the way home. Aside from the computer, what on earth had the intruders thought they would find that made it worth the time to rip the place to shreds? While the others ate leftover chicken she went online to check her bank accounts and change all her passwords.

She'd no sooner finished that task than her mother suggested a game of dominoes. The parents quickly cleared the dining table but Sam couldn't keep her mind on the game. Beau kept sending questioning glances across the table to her and Sam felt as if her head would burst with all the information she wanted to share with him.

"You two don't need to stay up with us old folks," Howard finally said. "Beau, quit seducing her across the table, just take her on upstairs. We'll play the TV loud enough that y'all don't have to worry about staying quiet."

Nina Rae's eyes went wide. "Howard!"

Oh, god, Sam thought. She felt her face redden.

"Samantha, your daddy's right. You two are supposed to be on your honeymoon. It's okay if y'all want to, um, turn in a little early."

If only they knew. Sam and Beau played out the final domino hand and practically raced up the stairs, suppressing laughter.

"As much as I wouldn't mind my father's little speculation to be true, I'm guessing that those eye-wiggles from your side of the table have more to do with our investigation," she said the minute they closed the bedroom door behind them.

"I finally remembered to check on those mobster types you spotted at the press conference, the ones we think might be connected to Jake's gambling debts." He kept his voice low. "One of my deputies saw them too, so I've had him going through databases to see if he recognized them. He found one, for sure, and a probable ID on the other. They're both from Las Vegas, so I can start there to get more info. Both have rap sheets for federal charges and there's a common denominator— they've both worked for a guy by the name of Kozark."

That sounded vaguely familiar. "Do we know anything about him?"

"Still checking. He's tied to Vegas too, suspected of lots of shady financial deals and loan sharking, but has managed to avoid being cited for anything more than a speeding ticket. I've got a bad feeling about the guy but no real information yet."

Sam nodded, wondering if the name Kozark should mean something to her.

"Your turn now," Beau said. "You can't drop a statement like 'I've got more' on me, like you did at Kelly's, and expect me to wait forever to learn what it is."

She sat cross-legged on the bed and told him about her visit with Doralee Calendar that afternoon—everything from the nervous tics that vibrated with the woman's insecurity over the divorce, to the fact that she'd gone so far as to watch Sam from afar, to the scene in the bar that had required the police.

"I'd like to know more about that," Beau said. He paced to the far end of the room and back. "My contact guy isn't on duty right now or I'd make a call and see how violent the fight really became."

Sam held up a finger and pulled out her phone.

"What's the number?"

"What are you doing?"

"The non-emergency police number?"

He recited it from memory.

"Hi," Sam said when someone at the police department picked up. "I'm with the *Gazette* and we're running a short piece on a disturbance at Murphy's Pub last Thursday night. I'd like to include some details."

She was put through to someone else and made the request again. Two minutes passed very slowly.

"Assault on one Jake Calendar? It's a matter of public record," said a man who sounded like he was rummaging through a stack of papers. "It's here. You can stop by and pick up a copy of the report."

"Oh, gosh, see I'm on deadline and my editor needs it tonight. I have most of what I need except the name of the person who assaulted him. Can you give me that much?"

"You all know the drill," the man said. "You're supposed to come by and get a copy."

"I know . . ." Sam sounded genuinely regretful. "But there's this deadline . . ."

"Hudson Moscowitz. That's all you're getting unless you come in." He hung up.

"Hudson Moscowitz?" She turned to Beau. "Is that a real person?"

"Hulk. That's what they call him. We've had him in a few times too. Real troublemaker, especially once he gets a few drinks in him."

"Well, this *Hulk* Moscowitz was the guy that tangled

with Jake Thursday night. I wonder what happened. Doralee only said there was 'a scene.' I can't really imagine Jake in a brawl, but then Kelly did see him get pretty angry with that poor guy who tried his impromptu audition. Maybe Jake had more of a temper than I ever knew."

"If I were betting on this one, I'd guess Moscowitz threw the first punch. He's like that."

"I saw Jake Friday morning. He didn't look battered."

"I'll get the full report," he said, "and we'll see what happened." He lowered himself into the armchair in the corner of the room and began pulling off his boots. "Meanwhile, want to hear about my little talk with Victor Garcia, aka Vic Valentino?"

"Absolutely." Sam leaned against the headboard and stretched out her legs, realizing that the morning's energy boost had completely worn off and she was on the verge of sleep.

"He may seem like a mild mannered kind of dweeb, but Mr. Valentino still has a lot of anger toward Jake Calendar for the way he publicly humiliated him."

Sam's interest perked up. "Really."

"Oh yeah. He went through the whole experience for me, maybe thinking that he could file some kind of charges against Jake."

"For smashing a cake, or for rejecting a really awful song?"

Beau shrugged. "The main thing is, he wanted to *press charges against Jake*. He didn't realize Jake was dead."

Oh. Sam let the information sink in, realizing she hadn't exactly told Vic the full story.

Beau continued. "It doesn't mean that he didn't deliver a doctored cupcake as a gift. He might have simply thought he would teach Jake a lesson by making him sick."

"Did you ask him that?"

"Didn't get the chance. I got a radio call right then and had to dash off. I left Mr. Valentino with the impression that I'd be back to take his formal statement. When he sees me he'll think he's getting back at Jake and I'll spring the news on him that he may just be a murder suspect."

Chapter 19

Sam woke the next morning to the barking of a dog and the realization that Beau was not in bed with her. Outside the window she heard his voice and Nellie became quiet. She peered through the curtains to see that the sun was up, revealing high clouds that had gathered overnight.

"Couldn't sleep," he said when she walked out to the back deck in her robe, carrying two coffee mugs. "I think your folks are still asleep, unless Nellie woke the whole household."

Sam patted the border collie, who wagged amiably at the sound of her voice. "Maybe she just wanted some attention."

They sat in the deck chairs but Sam felt anxious. It

was now the fourth day since their wedding would have happened. Four days in which she'd been a suspect. She didn't like the feeling.

"I suppose we could steer the police in the directions of all the other suspects we've found," she said. "They might drop the charges against me."

"It probably wouldn't do much good, sweetheart. They think they've got you and, knowing Pete Sanchez, that means they don't really want to muddy the water with a lot of other names."

"But it's not right!" She leaned forward in her chair. "It makes me want to scream."

He reached for her hand. "Me too. But I think we're better off gathering our evidence and putting together enough of it that they are forced to go after the real killer."

She nodded, wishing it could be otherwise.

"At the very least we're going to have lots of bits and pieces—maybe not enough to arrest someone else, but plenty that your attorney can present so much reasonable doubt that no jury would convict you."

"Beau, listen to yourself. It makes me sick to think that the words 'jury' and 'convict' can even be associated with me."

He set his mug down and stood up. "I'm sorry, darlin'. Come here."

She faced him and he wrapped his arms around her in the comforting, all inclusive hug she loved so well. Her breath was warm on his chest; his fingers ran through her hair as he nestled her close to him.

"It's all going to be fine," he murmured. "Just fine.

Don't you worry."

She felt hot tears sting at her eyelids and she squeezed them shut.

"Your mother's up. I can see her going into the kitchen," he said. "Just FYI."

She pulled back and looked into his eyes. "Thank you for being so good to me. I can't tell you how much it means that you're supporting me through all this."

"You're about to become my wife," he said with a smile. "I can't imagine *not* sticking by you. Even if your parents end up moving in."

She kicked at his boot with her slipper. "Not funny. That is *so* not happening."

Beau reached for their coffee mugs. "Here she comes."

The French door opened and Nina Rae stepped out. "Uh-huh," she was saying into the phone at her ear. "Well, don't you worry about it, honey. I'll put you on with your mama."

She handed the phone to Sam. "It's Kelly."

Sam stared at the phone and realized it was her own. *You answered my cell phone?*

"Kel? Everything okay?" Sam asked, turning away.

"Sure." Her voice sounded perky and entirely normal. "I was just telling Gramma that I might not see them today. That's what I was calling about, Mom. Do you think you could stop by the police station and get the copy of our report on the burglary? I have to work all day and the insurance company wants it faxed to them before five o'clock, if possible."

"No problem. I'll be out and about all day, I think."

She hung up and stuffed the phone into the pocket of her robe, realizing that she hadn't yet dreamed up the day's entertainment for her parents. She felt the beginning of a headache.

Beau was in the kitchen, breaking eggs into a bowl when she went inside, and her mother had gone back into the guest room. When she emerged a few minutes later it was with a grim look.

"Your daddy is coming down with a cold," she announced. "I knew it. Yesterday he ate lunch without using my little bottle of hand sanitizer. I *told* him this would happen." She opened the refrigerator and pulled out the orange juice.

In Sam's experience, when her mother told you something would happen you'd best go along with it. She went to the guest room where she found her father in bed, propped up with three pillows behind his back.

"Daddy? Mother says you're getting a cold. You feel like staying in bed this morning?"

"Not really," he grumbled, "but I will."

He breathed deeply and Sam thought he sounded clear enough.

"Here's your o.j. Howard. Now drink up," Nina Rae said, bustling into the room and turning the thermostat up another two notches.

He took the glass from her and gave Sam a subtle wink as he raised it to his mouth.

"Beau's making scrambled eggs and toast, if you feel like having some," she said.

"I'd better take his temperature first," Nina Rae said.

Sam went back to the kitchen. Nina Rae insisted on taking a tray to Howard, "so he won't be spreading his germs around" but considering that they'd been in contact with him already it seemed a little pointless. When Sam peeked in to tell him she needed to go into town to do some things he practically begged her to take her mother along.

Nina Rae dithered over the decision, torn between staying to wait on her husband hand and foot or go to the pharmacy and load up on remedies. When Howard insisted that he ought to start taking more vitamins, Sam found her mother waiting by the front door, ready to ride along.

"Now don't you pay attention to me," Nina Rae said as they passed the small artisan stands on the north edge of town. "I won't need but a minute at the pharmacy and I'll just ride along while you do your errands."

Sam smiled weakly across the console at her. How to describe all the things she'd been hoping to accomplish today?

"The best pharmacy in town is near the supermarket, Mother. I'm sure you can find whatever you want. But I'm going to stop off and get that police report for Kelly first."

She'd purposely been a little sketchy with the details about the break-in at Kelly's place, making it sound more like someone had picked up a few items from the front porch than the real chaos they'd found inside. Nothing could get her mother going on her you'd-better-move-back-to-Texas soapbox faster than believing that something dangerous had happened here in Taos. Sam parked in a shady spot and said she would be back in a couple of minutes.

It took her that long just to find out who to ask about the report and while the clerk went to pull the record and make the copy, a female voice rose from a nearby corridor. An officer came out, escorting Doralee Calendar.

"I can't believe you gave his things to someone else. I'm his *wife*," Doralee was saying, apparently not for the first time, judging by the expression on the officer's face. "Why didn't you call *me*?"

"Ma'am, I already explained that. The emergency contact number in Mr. Calendar's wallet listed his brother. It's procedure. The items have been claimed and there's nothing more I do for you."

Doralee looked ready to burst a vessel when she spotted Sam. It took about two seconds for her to switch directions and ask the favor.

"Sam," she said, "can you do anything about this?"

"Sorry, no." Kindnesses at the police department were hardly coming Sam's way this week.

Meanwhile the officer had escaped and Doralee had latched onto Sam.

"There's just so much official business to take care of when someone dies. I never realized . . . insurance, bank accounts, bills and things . . ." She waved a sheaf of papers toward Sam, as if that might make the bills go away.

"I'm sure it's tough."

"It doesn't help that he'd moved out. I don't even

have a key to that apartment where he went."

What part of "I'm divorcing you" didn't this woman get?

"Doralee, you probably just need to go home and let this new situation settle in. You'll get used to it in time and you'll build a new life for yourself."

Doralee gave Sam an impatient glare—she'd probably gotten the same advice from everyone she knew, including Jake. She stomped out.

The clerk returned with Sam's burglary report and handed it over.

Sam was all the way down the block when she remembered her phone call the previous evening to find out more about the altercation Jake had gotten into at Murphy's Pub. She could have picked up the report on that incident at the same time.

Her mother interrupted her train of thought. "Oh, Samantha! There's a drug store, right there."

Pointing out that the other store probably had a better selection would do no good. Sam made a quick right-hand turn and parked in front of the place her mother had spotted. While Nina Rae went inside, Sam dialed Beau's cell.

"I just missed a chance to get the police report on Jake's fight with that guy . . . what was his name?"

"Hulk Moscowitz. Don't worry about it. I can have it faxed to my office. Maybe we can meet up for lunch later and compare notes."

"I'm hoping to take Mother back out to the house so she can drive Daddy nuts instead of me. I'll give you a call." She looked up to see Nina Rae approaching the truck.

"Well, that little place didn't have hardly anything. Out of vitamin C and they didn't even carry the best brand of decongestant."

"We'll try another place," Sam said, her mind on getting the police report to Kelly.

She used Martyrs Lane as a shortcut to Camino de la Placita and headed toward Sweet's Sweets. Nina Rae said she would say hello to the girls at the bakery while Sam walked over to Puppy Chic. Kelly was up to her elbows with a sudsy little brown dog whose long hair lay in wet ropes down the sides of its face when Sam walked into the back room. The owner, Erica Davis-Jones, had a cocker spaniel on the clipping table and the dog was patiently allowing the shaver to take tufts of hair off its paws. About an acre of clipped blond hair already lay on the floor around the groomer's feet.

"How *are* you, Sam?" Riki asked, briefly taking her eyes off the dog.

"I have to say I'd be a lot better if Saturday had gone as planned, but overall I'm coping." She held up the police report. "This is your report, Kelly. I'll just set the page somewhere safe."

She found a spot on a high shelf well away from the hair and water.

"Did you and Jen sleep okay last night?" Sam asked Kelly.

"Having her over brought back memories of a lot of slumber parties. And without Mom at home."

She wiggled her eyebrows and the dog in the deep sink tried to make a break for it while her attention was elsewhere. "Bidgit! Stop that!" She got a better grip on the slippery critter. "But yeah, we slept. Didn't have the kind of up-all-night stamina we did when we were twelve."

Sam smiled at that memory.

"Yoo-hoo! Where *is* everyone?" Nina Rae's voice carried with megaphone clarity.

"One moment," Riki called out automatically.

"I better go," Sam said quickly. She walked toward the reception area but found her mother already on her way to the back room.

"Well, I better give my granddaughter a hug before I go," she said, pushing past Sam. "Kelly, hon, thank you so much for taking us on that beautiful drive yesterday. Your Grampa got a cold, but we had the best time. Woo—that little guy's all wet!"

Kelly reached for a towel to get the spray the dog had shaken across the room. Sam waited while her mother dabbed droplets from her silk blouse and then ushered her back out to the truck.

"Let's get to the pharmacy," she suggested, "and then I can drop you back at the house."

"Beau said something about getting together for lunch."

"Oh, did he?" Sam saw their chance to discuss the case flying out the window, unless she wanted the details to be headline news at the Cottonville Ladies Bridge Club next week. She put on her smile and drove south on Paseo.

"Now I don't want to mess up y'all's plans. I know you're real busy with all that police stuff. I can go back to the house right after lunch. Your daddy will be needing me for something by then anyway."

Sam pulled into the parking lot at the pharmacy where she'd originally intended to go. "Take your time, Mother. If you don't find what you need, the supermarket across the street has a lot of stuff too."

She speed-dialed Beau's number as Nina Rae walked toward the store.

"Just a heads-up. Mother thinks she's invited to lunch, so we'll have to be careful what we say about the case in front of her."

"Gotcha. Well, I've hit one roadblock already this morning. Went back to ask Vic Valentino what he knew about the cupcake. The guy's not as clueless as he appears. He found out that Jake's dead, that you were arrested for it, and that I'm looking out for you. He wouldn't tell me anything except to go talk to his lawyer."

Rats. The bad news was that they wouldn't get any voluntary info out of Vic; the good news was that his being so defensive definitely kept him on their suspect list. Plus, he knew the bakery and what they had to offer; it would have been a simple matter for him to get the cupcake. He seemed the kind of guy who would be more likely to sneak poison to an enemy than to confront him outright, especially a man of Jake's size and build. And the fact remained that he had motive; Jake had publicly humiliated him in his hometown where Vic's friends could easily have seen or heard of the incident.

The thoughts tumbled through Sam's brain until she spotted her mother coming toward the truck, a tiny paper sack in hand.

"Well, wouldn't you know it. They had the decongestant but not the cough syrup or the vitamins. I guess we'll have to go on to that other place you were talking about." Nina Rae fastened her seat belt. "It's just so frustrating shopping in a strange town. Back home I'd have called up Jim Ed at the Rexall and he'd have all this stuff gathered up for me before I got there."

You could go home any time and get right back into your routine. Sam bit at her lower lip as she backed out of the parking spot. A glimpse of Nina Rae clutching the little bag with her thin fingers brought her up short. Somewhere along the line, her mother had aged and it suddenly hit Sam that all the attempts to control the outcome of things . . . maybe that was only a frantic attempt to stop the clock and go back to the days when Mother was truly in charge of the family. Her push for the wedding might simply be every mother's desire to see things work out perfectly for her daughter. Didn't Sam want the same for Kelly? Weren't their wishes very much the same?

She swallowed hard as she pulled into the supermarket parking lot. They walked inside together and Sam steered her mother toward the vitamin aisle, picking up a bottle of Vitamin C for their own use before heading toward the produce section. While she was staring at the apples her phone rang.

"Darlin' I'm sorry I have to skip lunch with you ladies," Beau said. "A call came in, traffic accident north of Questa. I have to head up there."

"Okay. Call me when you get any news." She tried to put some cheer in her voice but inside felt frustration rise. Could they meet *any more* roadblocks in getting on with the investigation? Or was Sam, in her push to straighten out this situation, doing all the very things she didn't like about her mother?

Put it aside, she lectured herself. *Enjoy the day rather than chafing at the way things are going.*

They finalized their purchases and Sam chose a nice spot for lunch, a place with tables along the sidewalk. They ordered and Nina Rae commented on the variety of little galleries and shops in the area. Sam closed her eyes for a moment, wanting to follow her own advice and relax, but the fact was that she couldn't forget that she was still, in the eyes of the police, a murder suspect. She had to stay diligent.

Their lunches arrived and Nina Rae exclaimed over them. Sam chewed at the plain salad she'd ordered but her mind wandered, going over the list of suspects she and Beau were considering. Aside from the group from California, Vic Valentino was starting to look viable, the loan shark *had* uttered a threat, and they still didn't know how serious the altercation in the pub had gotten. Maybe Jake left that Hulk guy mad enough to come after him. Doralee might be a suspect too, except that she'd seemed more intent on keeping Jake married to her than getting rid of him. If anything, she would have probably wanted to harm Evie.

Which brought up another possibility. They could be going about this all wrong if Evie had been the real intended victim . . .

". . . did you?" Nina Rae's rambling narrative had apparently turned into a question.

"Sorry, Mother, I—"

"I know, honey." She reached over to pat Sam's knee. "You've got so much on your mind. Me asking about the flowers for your wedding was insensitive. I'm sorry."

Sam blinked away the sense of unreality. Wedding flowers and murder charges; a white gown and a jail cell; a string of suspects but no real leads . . . How had her life become so completely twisted around in only a week's time?

"Is it anything you want to tell me about?"

How could she get into the complexities of the situation without facing a lot of questions about Jake and the past? She shook her head. "Nothing all that important. Let's just enjoy our lunch."

The clouds seemed to have thickened, cooling the air. They quickly finished their salads and Nina Rae pulled cash from her purse.

"My treat," she said, reminding Sam of her mother's generous nature. "I just love the looks of that little shop across the lane there. Can we take a peek on the way back to the truck?"

"Sure. They've got some cute things; Kelly loves that place," Sam said as they walked away from the sidewalk café.

Before they reached the boutique, which sold purses, scarves and about a million little paper items like stationery and diaries, Sam's phone rang.

"Go ahead, Mother. I'll be right in." She noticed on the readout that it was Beau.

"Hey there. I'm at a lull in the action here, waiting for

a tow truck that's probably at least fifteen minutes away. I thought I'd tell you that I got the police report on that altercation at Murphy's Pub. It came in on the fax as I was walking out awhile ago."

"What's it say? Who started it?"

"No one seemed to know. According to three witnesses, Jake and Hulk Moscowitz had words and the next thing anyone knew a table was overturned and there was broken glass all over the place. The bartender called the cops before it could get worse."

"Well, Jake didn't have any marks on him the next day. Maybe he got the better of the Hulk?"

"It's possible. No one was taken away for medical care, but that doesn't mean he didn't limp out with some minor injuries—either to his body or his ego."

"I get the idea with this Hulk guy that an ego injury would hurt worse."

He chuckled. "Probably so."

"But would he wait until the next day and go to the trouble of poisoning a cupcake, just to get even? He sounds more like a flash-temper sort of guy."

"Yeah, I agree. I see him more likely to wait in a dark alley than to plan something in advance. Doesn't look like the police ever called him back in for more questions and no one filed charges."

"So we move Hulk whatshisname to the bottom of our list?"

"Most likely. Are you still with your mother?"

"I'm at the shopping arcade off Bent Street. Mother's in one of the shops." She moved a little farther from the door. "I'm just about ready to say screw the white dress and flowers and ceremony, let's just get the judge to marry us right away."

"Really? You know my opinion. I'd do it right now."

"Couple problems. I need to be sure my dad isn't really getting sick. I suspect it's like usual—he lays low for a day or so just to have a little quiet time. But what if? So, once we're sure about that, yeah. I'm ready. Well, except for the honeymoon. I can't leave until I get my passport back. So, no 'Ireland, here we come' just yet."

"Hang in there. We'll get this resolved."

"Call me again when you get back into town. Mother should be ready to go back to the house pretty soon."

A spur of the moment marriage in the judge's chambers would work for Sam and Beau, but she knew her mother would be severely disappointed to see the gown and cake and flowers and dinner go to waste. This wasn't over yet.

Chapter 20

Sam walked into the shop where her mother had disappeared, wondering what could possibly be taking so long. She found a middle-aged clerk standing near the north wall, arms out at her sides, scarves of four different colors draped over them.

"I just can't make up my mind, Samantha. What do you think?"

"I think any of them would look great on you, Mother."

"They're not for me—well, maybe just one. I'm getting one for you, one for Kelly, and one for Rayleen. Which colors go right for each of you?"

Sam had never been much good with scarves but there was no sense declining the gift. She chose the one she thought Zoë would most like. The blue-green weave would look nice with Kelly's eyes and she pointed it out, but she didn't have a clue about her sister. Nina Rae quickly narrowed it down and finalized her purchase.

"Now I suppose we'd best be getting back to your daddy. He'll be wanting his favorite lunch for when he's sick—I guess you call that 'comfort food'—a grilled cheese sandwich and tomato soup. I bought everything back there at the grocery so I'll get home and make it for him."

They arrived at the house to find Howard on the sofa with a sports channel on television, watching something that appeared to be a rerun of an old Super Bowl. A bowl of peanuts and glass of Coke sat on the coffee table, and he had the volume up so loud that he didn't immediately realize they had walked in.

"Hi, Daddy, we're home," Sam called out, in time for him to settle back into the cushions before Nina Rae could catch him pumping his fist at the screen.

"I'm making your favorite lunch, Howard. Don't go spoiling it with that junk food."

Sam crossed to the sofa and placed the back of her hand against his forehead. "You seem to be feeling better."

He wiggled his eyebrows at her. "Did you ladies have a nice morning out?"

Sam imagined that he purposely made his voice a little weak. Nina Rae went on about how much trouble they'd had finding all the right cold medications, reminding Sam that getting the parents back home to Texas needed to be a priority if she wanted to keep her sanity.

"I hope we don't have to get you to a doctor out here," Nina Rae said. "I'm not sure our insurance would cover it."

"We're not in a foreign country, Mama. And I'm not all that sick."

Insurance. Sam's mind zipped off in another direction while her parents kept up their habitual wrangling. Doralee Calendar had mentioned Jake's insurance. Was she still the beneficiary? Could that be the real reason she'd come to Taos to wheedle Jake out of going through with the divorce? And, since she hadn't been able to talk him out of stopping the divorce, maybe she'd decided there was more than one way to get that insurance money.

Sam went upstairs where she puttered for a few minutes, making the bed and tidying the master bath, trying to decide what she might do toward solving her predicament. She held the wooden box close to her chest, hoping some answers would miraculously appear. Outside, Nellie and Ranger let out their happy-barks and a glance out the window told her that Beau was coming up the driveway. She dashed down the stairs.

"Hey," he said, pulling off his Stetson with a sweep. "You girls are back from town. It was on my way back so I thought I'd stop in to see how you're feeling, Howard."

Sam thought her father looked as if he'd give anything to reverse the clock forty years and go to work for Beau's department. The two men chatted for a few minutes; Beau told a funny story about one of his traffic arrests before he stood up to leave again.

"I've thought of something else we should check out," she said, walking with Beau out to the front porch. Her dad had finished his cheese sandwich and settled back on the couch, while her mother returned to wiping counter tops in the kitchen. She told him about Doralee and the insurance.

"I can certainly do some checking on that," he said. "At the very least we can probably find out if their divorce was completely finalized and whether Doralee was still named as his beneficiary."

"Can I come along? I feel completely useless here, dusting the furniture and pacing the floor."

"I'll put you to work making phone calls," he warned.

"I'd love it."

"Better bring your vehicle, in case I get called out and can't get back until late."

Twenty minutes later Sam settled opposite Beau at his desk. He'd already been pecking away at his computer keys, once in awhile stopping to jot down a name or phone number.

"I had a thought," she said. "Earlier, when I saw Doralee at the police station, she had a bunch of documents with her. It didn't click with me then, but I remember seeing the logo for General Assurance Life. I'll bet that's the policy."

"They aren't going to give you any information. An unrelated party."

She bit at her lip. "I could say that Jake is my daughter's father and ask if she's one of the beneficiaries on the policy. She won't be, but maybe they'll tell me who is."

He looked skeptical. "You can't answer any of the security questions they're bound to ask."

"Okay, how about this? I'll call Tom Calendar and have him do it. He'll know enough of Jake's personal data that he can get through the questions. Legally, if the Doralee divorce was final, Tom probably is next of kin."

"Hey, it's worth a try."

She talked to Tom for a few minutes while Beau continued to pull data from the computer.

"He says he'll be glad to find out," she said.

"Come look at this." Beau turned his computer screen toward her. "Recognize this guy?"

She stared at the hard face. The blond man who'd approached Jake on the plaza while Sam was talking to him.

"Anthony Kozark," Beau said.

Sam recalled the few words she'd overheard. "I tell you, he sounded ominous when he made that remark about Jake getting a bad taco. In context, I could sure take that as a reference to poison."

Beau tapped at his notepad with a pencil. "I can't rule it out. But that seems pretty risky. It doesn't take a lot of cyanide to be fatal. And once the victim is dead, well, Kozark certainly wouldn't get his money then."

"Unless he thought Jake had already gotten the money from me . . . Jake might have told him that. Once they knew Jake was dead they could easily be the guys who ripped my house apart looking for it."

Beau picked up the phone and Sam listened to his end of the conversation. An old contact of his in Las Vegas, whom Sam had met a few months back, said he would stake out Tony Kozark's known haunts and pick him up for questioning. Toward the end of the conversation Beau uttered an "ugh" and made a face.

"What was that last bit about?" Sam asked as soon as he set the phone down.

"Kozark's nickname in Vegas—The Nail. Wanna know why?"

"I'm not sure."

"Because he's been known to use a nail gun to teach lessons to those who don't pay up. It's his signature tactic."

"Nail gun? My god!"

"Yeah. Ruskovik says last year they found some guy with his, um, private parts nailed to a wood floor. Says it's usually just fingers or wrists. But none of the victims will talk, much less testify in court, so the police have never been able to officially pin any of the attacks on him."

Sam felt a little queasy. "Oh wow. I almost feel like Jake was lucky."

"He might have agreed with you on that. Anyway, I'm liking this Kozark less and less. Poison doesn't seem like his style."

Sam nodded, trying to blur out the vision of the nail gun. Her phone rang.

"Hi, Sam. Tom Calendar here. I have some information for you. General Assurance looked up Jake's policy. The insurance is for three hundred thousand and Doralee is listed as sole beneficiary."

"Even if the divorce was final?"

"He hadn't changed it—so yeah, I guess so."

Sam thanked him and clicked off the call. She passed the information along to Beau.

"So it looks like the person who ends up better off with Jake dead really is Doralee," he said, tapping the pencil again. "I think I'd like to have a little chat with her. She's at the Taos Inn?"

Sam nodded.

"Let's go." He strapped on the heavy belt that made his uniform complete—sidearm in holster, spare magazine, nightstick and cuffs. The sight of it made Sam not mind her extra ten pounds quite so much.

The department cruiser covered the few blocks easily, other cars seeming to melt off to the sides of the road as Beau came up on them. He pulled into the hotel's parking lot and rolled up to the front door.

Amazing how much more cooperative desk clerks became when the county sheriff made the request, Sam thought. The fortyish woman eyed Beau appreciatively and nearly fell over herself to get the information he wanted.

"Ms. Calendar was in room one-nineteen," she said after a few taps at her keyboard. "But she checked out."

"When? I just saw her this morning." Sam blurted it out without thinking.

The clerk looked to Beau and realized he expected an answer to the question.

"Just before noon."

Sam looked up at Beau and he nodded toward the big double entry doors. They walked out.

"So Doralee is getting away," Sam said. "She'll go back to California, walk into that insurance office, and collect."

"She might be rightly entitled, Sam. But if not at least

we can slow her down."

He flipped on the lights and siren, getting them back to his office in half the time. He whipped into his assigned parking slot and keyed the code for the back door. At his desk he picked up the file he'd locked into a drawer and flipped it open. In a moment he'd punched in the number for General Assurance Life.

"Without a court order, I'm not sure this will stick," he whispered to Sam while he waited on Hold. "But it might keep Doralee from cashing a check before we can put together the rest of the evidence."

No kidding. Put a shred of doubt into an insurance company's files and you were bound to see delays.

His attention snapped to the telephone. "Yes, this is Sheriff Beau Cardwell in Taos County, New Mexico . . ."

Chapter 21

"I need to get to the bakery and see how things are going," Sam said after Beau had finished the call.

She aimed an air kiss his direction and went out to her truck, zipping her jacket against the cooling afternoon air. The wind had picked up and the clouds were definitely darkening. She felt a sense of relief that they'd figured out a way to stop Doralee from cashing in on Jake's death, but random thoughts still nagged at her.

Why didn't Doralee go right back to California after killing Jake? Why wait around town and try to claim his few personal possessions if she had a $300,000 payout coming? But still, she was their most viable suspect.

Sam made the turn onto Camino de la Placita and slowed for traffic at the next four-way stop. A grey fuzz appeared near the hood of her truck.

Two figures.

She blinked and they were gone. Two phantom-like figures had appeared to her in Jake's hotel room. She distinctly remembered them. What did they mean?

She squeezed her eyes shut to get the vision back but a horn beeped behind her. She moved ahead until her turn came and she went through the intersection. A block later she was at Sweet's Sweets, pulling into her customary spot in the alley behind the shop.

"Hey there," Becky said when Sam walked in. "Didn't expect to see you today."

Sam took a moment to ask how each of them was doing and to check the stack of order forms. Two new wedding cakes and five birthday parties. Jen had done a good job of noting details and providing sketches; she would surely be able to handle whatever came through the door while Sam and Beau were away. *If* they ever got away.

Out front in the sales room, the display cases were appropriately depleted. By late afternoon Sam liked to see a couple dozen cookies and no more than two or three big desserts— assorted pies or cakes; the after-school kids and a few busy moms who needed a quick dessert would finish those off. A big part of their success depended on everything being made fresh every day and Sam and her crew prided themselves on estimating their needs for each day of the week. She wiped up a few spills from the beverage bar while Jen sold chocolate chip cookies to three girls in Catholic school uniforms.

"Shall I tally up the drawer or do you want to?" Jen asked. She hit a key on the register to show Sam the sales for the day.

"Looks good. You guys don't seem to need me around here." She chuckled and gave Jen a pat on the shoulder. "I better get back to the house and see what my parents are up to. You can go ahead and write up the deposit and get it to the bank tomorrow, if you don't mind."

Jen nodded, turning to the sound of the little bells at the front door. Sam registered a middle aged woman whose eyes seemed intent on the one remaining apple tart. She turned back to the kitchen just as her phone vibrated in her pocket.

"Got a second?" Beau asked. "I heard back from Ruskovik in Las Vegas. It doesn't look like Kozark could be our guy. He was back in Vegas the day Jake died."

"But I saw him—"

"Southwest Airlines had him leaving Albuquerque on a noon flight that put him into Vegas before two p.m."

"And Jake died in the late afternoon." She ran through scenarios—Kozark delivering the cupcake and then leaving town, having one of his goons do it—but nothing really fit. Neither the style nor the timeframe.

"Anyway, he's out as a suspect."

"Which really leaves Doralee as the most likely."

"I'm almost looking forward to meeting with Pete Sanchez. The guy is a pretentious jerk and this time I can blow about a hundred holes in his case."

The memory of the two smoky figures went through Sam's head again. One had seemed slight, like Doralee.

So, who was the other one? "Something about Doralee bothers me. I just can't quite put my finger on it yet."

"Well, if you don't mind waiting, I guess tomorrow's fine to face down Sanchez. Let me know if it comes to you. I'll see you at home soon?"

"Yep, almost on my way." It would only take a few minutes to place an order for the supplies that Becky had neatly written on a list.

Julio nearly had all the baking pans and utensils washed, she noticed, and Becky set a finished cake into the fridge and walked over to the desk. Sam showed her the website where she ordered specialty items—in case someone came in with a desire for an art deco bridal cake topper or something. Otherwise, she told her assistant, their supplies of flour, sugar and other staples should tide them over for the coming weeks.

"Sam?" Jen's voice came over the intercom. "There's somebody on line one that won't talk to anyone but you. She sounds really upset."

Great. Just what she needed at five minutes to closing, a customer who'd probably forgotten that her kid's birthday party started in an hour. She gave a sigh and picked up the phone.

"Samantha Sweet here."

"Sam? It's Evie Madsen," the tearful voice said. "I need help."

Chapter 22

And I'm your mother? Sam almost cut Evie off but something in the girl's voice sounded truly desperate.

"What's happened? Where is Tustin?"

"He blew a gasket earlier—started screaming at me. He pulled off the street at this coffee place and left me there. I didn't even get my purse." Her voice rose, thin and reedy.

"Which coffee shop? Maybe you could ride the town trolley back to your hotel."

"No! I can't go back there. He might be there. I—I don't know what to do, Sam. Can you come get me?" The girl choked back a sob.

Sam searched for any other answer, someone she could

send to help Evie out of her situation. Social services, a battered women's shelter, the police? Sam didn't exactly have inroads with any of them. And she had to admit she was curious why the pair hadn't left town already.

"I'll come over. Which coffee shop is it?"

"They closed and the manager made me go. I went next door to a bridal shop and hid in the back room. When the girl who worked here left, that's when I decided I could call you."

Sam knew the place—Beautiful Bridals, right next to Java Joe's Joint. "I can be there in about ten minutes and I'll come to the back door."

"Thank you, Sam, I'm so sorry, I—"

"It's okay. Just sit tight." She hung up and debated calling Beau. No point, really. She would drive Evie to the Greyhound lobby and buy her a ticket for Los Angeles. After that, the girl was on her own. She pictured the young woman, tall and proud as she stood on all those various red carpets, now riding the bus to the coast. Would she even go for such a plan? Well, Sam would deal with that when they met.

Outside, the sky had darkened ominously and fat raindrops began to smack her windshield as she turned onto Paseo del Pueblo Sur.

Beautiful Bridals had soft pink night lights in the front windows where long gowns were displayed on three impossibly thin, size zero mannequins. Sam held her stomach in and grumbled at them as she passed the shop and took a driveway that led to the service entrances of the few businesses in the little strip center.

The metal door she was looking for was painted pink. She parked the truck under the one-bulb light fixture above it, picked up her heavy flashlight, and stepped out into the rain. Wind whipped at her jacket as she rapped at the door.

"Evie? It's Sam. Open up. I'm getting soaked out here."

Locks rattled and the door opened a smidge.

"Evie, come on. Let's go."

No response.

"Evie." Sam stepped into the darkness and pushed the heavy door shut with her butt. She went on hyper-alert and tightened her grip on her flashlight. Ahead of her she saw the outline of a doorway, similar to that in her own shop, separating the small stockroom from the larger sales area. She scanned the stockroom with her flashlight. The two areas were separated by a filmy curtain. The sales room glowed softly with the pinkish window display lights. "Evie, if you don't show yourself I'm leaving. Right this minute."

A loud sob sounded ahead of her and Evie's silhouette emerged from the dark. "Sorry, Sam. I had to be sure you were alone." She wiped at her nose with one hand.

Sam shone her light toward the voice. Evie squinted her tear-swollen eyes shut. Trails of mascara stained her face. A red knot stood out on one cheek.

"He did that?" Sam said, moving the light out of her eyes. The young woman nodded.

There went the idea of simply putting her on a bus. No way would Evie want to be seen until she'd had time to work on the damage.

"Come here, blow your nose." Sam handed Evie a tissue and searched the room for a chair or desk but the space was pretty well filled with large cardboard cartons.

A flimsy metal shelf against one wall held rhinestone tiaras and some generic white silk bouquets. She peeked into the other room where a sales desk at least afforded a chair.

"Sit down out there. If we don't turn on any lights, no one will notice us. We can talk a minute and make a plan for you." She went into the tiny restroom and wet three paper towels with water, carrying them out to Evie.

"I assumed you two had left town yesterday, after I refused to give Tustin any money," she said, cupping Evie's chin and dabbing at the red welt on her cheek.

"He wouldn't give up on the idea. Of the money." Evie blinked a couple of times. "Said we *had* to get it before we left."

A vision of her slashed mattress popped into Sam's head. She remembered Beau's findings on the producer's financial state. It was a wonder the hotel had accepted one of his maxed out credit cards. No point in asking Evie about it though.

"With everything coming together for the show, I guess there were even more people wanting payments for things, huh? The audition venues, the judges, contracts to be satisfied . . ."

Evie snorted. "The show was a sham. Right from the start, there *was* no show."

Sam stood up and leaned back against the desk.

"What? But the auditions . . ."

"Never happened."

"The celebrity judges . . .?"

"*I* was the biggest celebrity who ever spoke to Tustin. I watched him make call after call. Nobody in Hollywood would talk to him."

Sam let that information tumble around in her mind.

"How did Jake Calendar come into this?"

Evie took the paper towels from Sam and pulled a small cheval-style mirror across the desk so she could look into it. In the dim light she began working on the mascara smudges with a fingertip.

"Jake and Tustin were made for each other. Two of the biggest bullshit artists on the scene." She stared up at Sam. "In Hollywood, that's saying a lot."

Sam glanced toward the front windows where traffic flowed normally out on Paseo. Lights reflected crazily off the wet pavement. No one had noticed them.

"Jake had convinced Tustin that his band was on the verge of a huge hit, that they had a major recording contract and were about to release an album. He said that Tustin could feature them on *You're The Star* and see to it that they made it to the finals to help launch this album into, like, major sales. Plus, Jake wrote up this contract making himself artistic director of the show and it said he would get, like, this major percentage of the profits."

"Why would Tustin go along with that?"

"*Because*, Jake said he could get all this money."

"From me."

"Well, *yeah*." She finished with her right eye, doubled

the paper towel over and started on the left. "The joke was on both of them."

The picture became clear. Tustin would get nonexistent money and Jake would get a nonexistent contract from a nonexistent television hit show. They say you can't con a completely honest person, that there's always an element of greed in the picture somewhere, the lure of something for nothing. Tustin and Jake both had that mentality and the two had conned each other.

Evie stared into the mirror, rechecking her makeup repair job.

"So things went bad and Tustin wanted to be rid of Jake?"

Evie's gaze went to her lap.

"Evie? What happened to Jake?"

She started to stand up and push past, but Sam laid a hand on her shoulder. "Sit. Tell me. Now."

"Jake figured out the show was bogus when he told Tustin that he couldn't get you to give him the money. They had this huge, screaming fight at the hotel the day before the press conference. Tustin told me he was scared that Jake would tell everything to the press and blow his whole plan apart. I guess he thought he could still get the money from somewhere."

"Wait a minute—you said the fight was at the hotel? I thought Tustin didn't arrive in Taos until the day of the press conference."

Evie's perfect little eyebrows pulled together in the middle. "No . . . he was here before."

"How badly did Tustin want Jake out of the picture?

Did he threaten to kill him?"

Evie's eyes darted back and forth as she tried to come up with a story.

"Tell me the truth." Sam put all the force of motherhood into her voice. "This minute."

"He only wanted to make Jake sick. So he couldn't leave the room and do the press conference. Tustin could tell the story like he wanted to, without Jake contradicting him. I didn't mean to put so much—" Her mouth slammed shut.

"So much what, Evie?" Sam stepped closer. "Did *you* put the poison in the cupcake?"

"Just a little, I swear."

"My god, Evie, it doesn't take very much of that stuff. You killed him."

"I didn't! Let me tell it all." She began to twist the paper towels to shreds. "Tustin came in and asked me how I planned to make Jake sick. I showed him how I'd made a small hole in the cupcake and then smoothed the frosting back over to cover it up. He kept looking at the box of Ratzout, there on the desk in Jake's room."

Two smoky grey figures. She saw them again with clarity. One at a time, both Evie and Tustin had added poison to the cupcake.

"He didn't think Jake would get sick enough, I guess." Evie's lower lip began to tremble.

"You need to tell all of this to the police," Sam said, covering her anger with as much gentleness as she could force into her voice. "I'll take you to the station to talk to them."

Evie squirmed in her chair, glancing toward the gowns on display. At that moment a flash of light threw the room into brilliant clarity. A split second later the storefront windows exploded.

Chapter 23

Mannequins flew. Racks of white dresses billowed like sea foam over the hood of the car that sent the place into pandemonium. One headlight shattered and the other shone awkwardly at the intersection of wall and ceiling, highlighting a row of plastic heads wearing veils that had been knocked cockeyed. The engine sputtered and died.

A burst of vile curses, mostly beginning with F, reverberated through the chaotic room as Tustin Deor emerged from the car. Apparently, he'd come alone. His hair stuck out at wilder angles than normal and the black jacket hung off one shoulder. His face was a mask of fury.

"Evie, you stupid c—"

He hadn't finished the thought when he noticed that Sam had her phone in hand.

"Drop it!" he shouted.

She stared at him, trying to think what to say to calm him down.

"I said drop it!" His lips straightened into a narrow line of determination and he raised a gun.

She dropped the phone onto a pile of white satin.

"I drove around Java Joe's, baby, looking for you. Saw that red pickup truck out back here." His attention was on Evie, the red mark on her cheek making a stark slash of color against the white of her skin in the glaring light. He aimed the gun at her, holding it sideways in that ridiculous posture Hollywood had adopted as cool. Evie's face went another shade lighter.

"Tustin, you don't want to do this," Sam said, working the tremble out of her voice.

"Really. Evie, what did you tell her?" His eyes bored like hot embers. He took a step closer. "Evie. *What* did you tell her?"

Sam stole a sideways glance at Evie, who looked about ready to keel over. *Think, Sam. Stay cool.*

He took two more steps.

From twenty feet away he might actually hit one of them, despite his awkward hold on the gun and complete inability to sight down the barrel. Sam thought to her days as a kid in Texas, where Uncle Chub had taken her to the shooting range many times, and to the times in Alaska where everyone carried a sidearm as protection against bears. Tustin clearly didn't know what he was doing. But even an idiot could get lucky, especially at this range. She still didn't want to miss her own wedding.

Beside her, Evie whimpered.

"All of it," Sam said. "She told me everything."

She kept her eyes on the gun. *If he squeezes any tighter, start moving. Make it difficult.* She wanted to tell Evie what to do but there was no way.

"You conned Jake into thinking he would get famous from the show. But he couldn't come up with the money. You broke into my house looking for it, then you decided to . . ."

The gun lowered just a little.

"Your house?" He seemed genuinely puzzled.

She saw her chance and ducked, racing low, right at him. She grabbed the small mirror and smacked it against his forearm. The gun went flying. She barreled into his legs and he landed on his back, the air whooshing from his lungs. Before he could react, Sam straddled him and sat hard on his stomach.

"Evie! Grab my phone—speed dial number one on it. Now!"

Tustin was having a hard time breathing. Take that, you scrawny little fool, she thought. She lifted her weight just enough to allow him one deep inhalation.

"Hand it to me, Evie, and come stand by his car." Without taking her eyes off Tustin's face she took the phone.

"Beau, I've got him." She told him where they were and within three minutes sirens began to approach.

Beau's cruiser was soon joined by two from the Taos

PD. Tustin started to protest about brutality but the facts were evident—his car through the window and his gun lying on the floor hardly made him look like an innocent victim. The police slapped cuffs on Tustin and dragged him to his feet. Sam hastily explained that they needed to take Evie along in the second car, for which she earned a glare.

"Sorry," she told the girl, "but these guys have to sort it all out." Evie would get some kind of accessory charge but only a court could say how firm a sentence either of them would end up with.

"Afraid you're in for more questioning," Beau said. The two of them stood off to the side of the chaotic scene. "I doubt either of those two will tell the same story at the station that they told you. And I don't care what Sanchez says, I'm going to be there with you."

"I've got some questions of my own," she said, describing Tustin's look of uncertainty when she mentioned the break-in at her house.

"I may have the answer for you on that one. Kozark's men. Apparently, Thursday night Jake blabbed about you being his source for money—I got the sense that someone was aiming the nail gun at his hand at the moment. Kozark must have gotten on that flight to establish his alibi, while his goons stayed behind to look for the money."

The owner of Beautiful Bridals arrived as the first police cruiser was pulling away, a middle aged woman who immediately went hysterical when she saw the damage to her shop. Beau offered to call a deputy to provide security until her insurance adjuster could take a look. While he made that call, Sam phoned Mark Nelson and told him she would be talking to the police. He didn't sound happy to be dragged out at nine p.m. after a long day in court, but he told her to wait for him.

Both hands were straight up on the clock in the police station when Sam walked out. She'd related the whole story, and Evie managed to fill in a few of the blanks. One of Tustin's flunkies had purchased the cupcake but it was Evie's idea to leave it as a gift at the hotel desk, so Jake wouldn't know who to blame after he became ill.

Mark Nelson had to get a little pushy with Pete Sanchez, but finally the charges against Sam were dropped. The energy from the box had faded long ago and she wanted nothing more than to fall into bed.

Even so, a little tune ran persistently through her head. "I'm getting married in the morning . . ."

Chapter 24

Actually, the morning became filled with a mad scramble to get the wedding back on track. Dress, cake, flowers and a hasty plan to come up with food. Phone calls to friends that required too much explanation, but everyone quickly changed plans and agreed to be at Zoë's place at six o'clock that night.

Zoë and Darryl went all-out with the garden. Golden fairy lights twinkled in the twin blue spruce trees and across the top of the pergola. The storm had passed during the night, leaving everything fresh and scented with pine. Candles flickered in the cool evening air, casting faces in a soft glow.

On the flagstone patio, vines of brilliant red crape myrtle intertwined with short oak boughs; clusters of autumn-toned asters, daisies and chrysanthemums topped a long white-clothed table. Tiny candles interspersed the floral arrangements with constellations of light. Gold-trimmed china settings for twelve lined the table and a caterer's helpers waited discreetly in the kitchen. A side table held Sam's elaborate cake, none the worse for being saved an extra few days.

Kelly adjusted folds in Sam's veil. "Mom, you are the most beautiful bride I've ever seen."

Sam's eyelids prickled. "Don't get me started. I don't have the faintest idea how to repair smudged eye makeup." She pressed her lips together and stared at her reflection in the mirror. The champagne silk, the lace, the pearls . . . and the fit was perfect. At last.

"Everyone's out there, waiting for the star of the show. Beau looks so good in that tux," Kelly said, peering through the drapes in Zoë's sitting room. "Gramma's turned around in her seat, staring toward the house." She glanced back at Sam. "All I have to do is open this door."

Sam took a deep breath and picked up her bouquet. "Ready."

The door swung inward and Kelly stepped out in her long crimson dress, wearing the silver bracelet Sam had given her, carrying her own small bouquet from Zoë's garden. Sam gave her a ten-step lead and followed. And there was Beau, smiling with a bit of awe. She didn't notice anyone else—not the friends, the parents or the judge who'd agreed to come on such short notice—she only saw Beau.

Later, she barely remembered saying the vows, only

that the words were heartfelt and that their voices came out sincerely and confidently as they promised to love each other forever. When they exchanged rings Sam marveled at the warmth in Beau's hands.

"I love you, darlin'," he whispered right before he kissed her.

Now, seated at the midpoint along the dining table, candlelight warming the faces around her, Sam raised her glass.

"To wonderful friends and dear family. Thank you for sharing this evening with us."

Glasses clinked around the table and then Nina Rae pushed her chair back and stood up. "Samantha Jane, and our dear Beau. We are all so very happy for you. We were disappointed that the rest of the Sweet clan were not able to stay longer, but your Uncle Buster arranged a special surprise for you." She turned to her husband. "Howard, where is that thing?"

Howard reached under the table and brought out a small black case. He searched the group for a moment. "Kelly, come here sweetie. You know I don't know a dang thing about these computers."

Sam and Beau exchanged a puzzled look. Kelly took the case from her grandfather and unfolded it, revealing a tablet device. A few murmured words between them and Kelly tapped the screen a few times.

"Hey, Uncle Buster. You're on here live?" She said to the screen.

"You're darn tootin' I am," came the hearty voice. "Hold the screen up to your mama and let me tell her somethin'."

Sam didn't breathe for a few seconds, wondering what was up.

"Sammy and Beau. Everbody's sent you a greeting. Just touch that little button thingy at the bottom of the screen and you'll see 'em. We got the whole fam-damly for you two."

It was true. Each of the Sweet family who'd come for the wedding last weekend had recorded a short video greeting. The guests crowded behind Sam's chair to watch.

Bessie and Chub came on first. "Are we on?" Bessie asked, looking around the room, which Sam recognized as their living room in Tulsa. "I can't tell if the camera's on, Chub."

"It's on," he said, edging his eyes toward her but not turning way from the camera. "See the red light? Now just say something to Sammy and Beau." He cleared his throat. "Samantha and Beau, your Uncle Charles here. Uh, we just want to wish you both all the very best on your wedding day, and uh . . ."

"Oh let me say it," Bessie interrupted. "Sammy, I know you'll just be the most beautiful bride and I know you two are gonna be as happy as two little birdies in a nest and we're just so happy for you!" Her voice came out bright and high-spirited, and Sam wondered if she'd indulged in a glass or two of wine before getting up the nerve to do this.

"Have a happy life together!" they said in unison, apparently at the prompting of someone behind the camera.

Their film clip ended and there was a moment of fuzz before her cousin Willie came on.

"Well, shoot," she said, "I don't know how to do this darn thing and besides, I've gotta get back out to the barn and feed them—oh, really? You're recording already?" She looked directly at the camera for the first time. "Hey Sam, hey Beau! It was so great to visit your place and meet your horses and the dogs and all . . . and I just want you guys to have a great life together, and Sam I sure hope that stupid stuff with the police is finally done." She glanced sideways and back. "I shouldn't have said that last part. You two just keep going strong, okay? I'm glad you finally got to have your wedding."

Sam and Beau grinned at each other. He scooted his chair closer to hers and draped one arm over her shoulders while holding her right hand with his.

Rayleen came on the screen next. "Boys! Get yourselves over here!" She glanced up at the camera "Sammy and Beau, ya'll are such a cute couple and I sure hope ya'll have as great a marriage as Joe Bob and me." She kept her eyes forward but stretched out a hand to pull her husband into the picture. Joe Bob grinned and wished them a happy honeymoon. The two teens ended the greeting with a bored "Hey, dude. Stay cool."

When the recorded greetings were finished, Buster came back on. Lily sat beside him, her eyes full of warmth. "Sammy, I see that you look beautiful in your dress and I'm so happy for you, honey."

Buster piped up again. "Ya'll are gonna have a great life together, and if you ever need advice on where to invest your money for a good little retirement nest egg, I got just two words for you—oil futures!"

Sam burst out laughing and Beau was having a hard time keeping a straight face as they thanked him and shut down the connection.

"I have to say that was . . . very nice of them," Zoë said as she gave Sam's shoulders a squeeze.

"So," said Rupert, returning to his seat across the table. "what's the latest on the honeymoon plans?"

Sam had nearly forgotten. She looked at Beau.

He turned to her and reached for the inside pocket of his jacket. "I have a little wedding gift for you, my darlin' Samantha." He pulled out a small blue booklet. "We are on our way to Ireland tomorrow," he said.

"But I never called the lawyer back. What about our tickets?"

"I did that. He is thrilled for you and says you have a wonderful surprise waiting for you on the Emerald Isle."

What would it be, Sam wondered, running her fingers over the embossed gold lettering on her passport. Money? Property? Or simply a wonderful experience? She couldn't imagine anything better than what she had right here. Around the table her friends were smiling and enjoying their meal; her family—scattered though they were—shared a bond, although sometimes a bit wacky; her wedding had turned out to be everything she wanted. And there was Beau, his arm draped over the back of her chair, his ocean-blue eyes occasionally acknowledging the others but mainly . . . mainly his attention was all for her.

Discover all of Connie Shelton's mysteries!

THE CHARLIE PARKER SERIES

Deadly Gamble
Vacations Can Be Murder
Partnerships Can Be Murder
Small Towns Can Be Murder
Memories Can Be Murder
Honeymoons Can Be Murder
Reunions Can Be Murder
Competition Can Be Murder
Balloons Can Be Murder
Obsessions Can Be Murder
Gossip Can Be Murder
Stardom Can Be Murder
Phantoms Can Be Murder
Buried Secrets Can Be Murder
Legends Can Be Murder

Holidays Can Be Murder - a Christmas novella

THE SAMANTHA SWEET SERIES

Sweet Masterpiece
Sweet's Sweets
Sweet Holidays
Sweet Hearts
Bitter Sweet
Sweets Galore
Sweets, Begorra
Sweet Payback
Sweet Somethings
Sweets Forgotten
The Woodcarver's Secret

Connie Shelton is the *USA Today* bestselling author of the Charlie Parker mysteries and the Samantha Sweet mystery series. She has taught writing, is the creator of the Novel In A Weekend™ writing course, and was a contributor to *Chicken Soup for the Writer's Soul*. She and her husband live in northern New Mexico.

Sign up for Connie's free email mystery newsletter at
www.connieshelton.com
and be eligible for monthly prizes, notices about free books, and all the latest mystery news.

Contact by email: connie@connieshelton.com
Follow Connie on Facebook, Twitter, and Pinterest